YOU CAN'T SIT with US

MEAN GIRL MAKEOVER

BOOK 2

By
NANCY RUE

THOMAS NELSON
Since 1798

NASHVILLE   MEXICO CITY   RIO DE JANEIRO

You Can't Sit with Us
© 2014 by Nancy Rue

Published in Nashville, Tennessee, by Tommy Nelson. Tommy Nelson is
an imprint of Thomas Nelson. Thomas Nelson is a registered trademark of
HarperCollins Christian Publishing, Inc.

Tommy Nelson titles may be purchased in bulk for educational, business,
fund-raising, or sales promotional use. For information, please e-mail
SpecialMarkets@ThomasNelson.com.

ISBN-13: 978-1-4003-2371-5

Library of Congress Cataloging-in-Publication Data

Rue, Nancy N.
You can't sit with us / by Nancy Rue.
pages cm. -- (Mean girl makeover ; book 2)
Summary: Ginger Hollingberry, a new sixth grader at Gold Country Middle
School, relies on her faith and friends when she is bullied for being different by
the "queen bee" of GCMS, Kylie Steppe, and her so-called Wolf Pack, not only at
school but twenty-four hours a day through social networking.
ISBN 978-1-4003-2371-5 (paperback)
[1. Cyberbullying--Fiction. 2. Bullying--Fiction. 3. Individuality--Fiction. 4.
Middle schools--Fiction. 5. Schools--Fiction. 6. Single-parent families--Fiction.
7. Christian life--Fiction.] I. Title. II. Title: You cannot sit with us.
PZ7.R88515You 2014
[Fic]--dc23
    2014024948

Printed in the United States of America
14 15 16 17 18 19 RRD 6 5 4 3 2 1

In memory of my friend Kay Tallerico, who always kept the power to be herself.

Chapter One

In one week, my whole life changed.

Okay, not my whole *entire* life. I still lived with my dad and my brother, I still didn't have a cell phone, and I still had red hair that started to look like shredded carrots if I didn't wash it, like, every ten minutes.

I guess I should say my *school* life changed. When you're twelve and in sixth grade, school practically *is* your life.

In the seven days before that Thursday, no one had told me I was annoying.

In those one hundred sixty-eight hours, nobody had stuck gum in my hair or laughed right in my face or whispered, "I hate Gingerbread," when they passed me in the hall.

In those ten thousand and eighty minutes, I'd gone to the restroom between classes and nobody had harassed me, and I didn't have to go there at lunchtime to eat my sandwich in a stall. I'd even gone to my locker and not freaked out because there *might* be moldy cookies in there.

For those I-don't-how-many seconds, I wasn't that Ginger girl everybody was mean to.

Now I wanted to yell, "Woo-hoo!" and grin all goofy all the time, but my brother, Jackson, would have said, "Do you have gas or what?"

So on Thursday, March 12, when Mrs. Zabriski announced that the health part of P.E. was over and we would now be working with her husband, *Coach* Zabriski, I was the first to go, "Woo-hoo!" Actually I was the *only* one to go, "Woo-hoo!" Which was strange because I *wasn't* the only one who considered Mrs. Z to be their most unfavorite teacher.

Our other five sixth-grade teachers upheld this Code we had signed, which said we had to "respect the dignity of every human being." But Mrs. Zabriski . . . let's just say she let Kylie Steppe and her, um, mean-girl friends be just snarky enough to almost *dis*respect the dignity of every human being. Especially my friends and me. The Tribelet.

Like, just then, as we were all filing out of the health classroom, Kylie turned her head so her little splashy brown bob swung into her blue-with-gold-specks eyes. She brushed it away like she was all irritated with it and looked at Tori, the leader of our Tribelet—and my friend—and said, "Nice *shirt*."

That would have sounded like a compliment if Kylie's lip hadn't been curled all up to her nostrils like something smelled bad. Actually, something did because the BBAs (the boys who were always *b*urping or *b*elching or doing disgusting things with their *a*rmpits) were all around her, and the most disgusting thing *about* their armpits was the gross odor.

Anyway, Tori, who in my opinion had a way cuter bob than Kylie because it was chocolate brown and thick and she didn't use it like a weapon, just looked down at her Einstein hoodie sweatshirt and said, "Thanks. I like it."

Kylie nudged Riannon with her elbow, and Riannon's green eyes got all close together, and she said, "OBviously. You wear it practically every single day."

I could've pointed out that Riannon shouldn't talk because she wore those green contact lenses every day, and they looked totally fake. But saying stuff like that wasn't in the Code, and besides, I also felt like I tasted whatever they were smelling when I did.

The line going down the hall toward the outside door spread out, but of course the Tribelet stayed together: Tori, Ophelia, Mitch, Winnie, and me.

"I'm scared of Coach Zabriski," Winnie said.

I almost didn't hear her because everything about her was sort of feathery, including her almost white hair and her voice. I just knew she'd be saying it. She was pretty much scared of everything.

Ophelia, on the other hand (I liked thinking things like "on the other hand"), got into it when something scary was about to happen, although I still didn't get what was so bad about Coach Zabriski. When I moved to Grass Valley and started at Gold Country Middle School, we were already doing health with Mrs. Z, so I didn't know him.

"Do you think he'll make us run laps again?" Ophelia said as we passed through the double doors to the schoolyard. Her eyes got as big and round as two Oreos, and she pulled the pink tie thingy out of her braid. Butter-colored hair unraveled down her back.

"What did you do that for?" Mitch said. She never understood Ophelia and her hair. Mitch's own was brown and spiky and short, and she liked being called Mitch instead of Michelle. Mitch was tough, and she could be as prickly as her own hairdo. She once punched a kid in the face for calling her brother retarded, but she didn't do that kind of thing anymore—not since the Code—but nobody forgot that she *could*.

Anyway, back to Ophelia's hair, which the March wind picked up and swirled in the air as we headed for the fenced-in area where everybody else was going.

"I want it to look dramatic if we have to report him for student abuse," she said.

"Is she serious?" Mitch said to me.

"Oh, yeah," I said. I was sure my grin was goofy—I was glad my brother wasn't standing there—but I couldn't help it. Nobody ever used to ask my opinion about anything, so when they did now it was woo-hoo worthy.

"All right, people, let's move it!" a voice bellowed (that's the only word for it) from the other side of the fence.

It belonged to a short guy with that kind of hair that's cut flat on the top. I couldn't be sure, but it looked like he dyed what there was of it blond. I never knew guys did that.

Mitch grabbed my arm and broke into a stampede kind of run, but Coach yelled, "You know better than that, Iann."

"Wish he'd make up his mind," Mitch muttered to me.

"I know, right?" I said.

Mitch grunted. That was Mitch for "you're okay."

It was good to be okay.

Coach Zabriski (on the other hand) didn't seem to think that *anybody* was okay. He stood in front of this big wooden frame thing with thick, knotted ropes hanging down from it. The way he had his arms—which kind of reminded me of two big hams—folded across his chest and the way his whole forehead came down over his eyes like the hood on Tori's sweatshirt, I wondered if he was about to use those ropes to tie us up. Beside me, little Winnie whimpered. She did that a lot.

When our whole class was bunched up in front of him, Coach said, "I see we have some 'tudes in this group."

I raised my hand. He lifted his chin at me, which I guessed meant he was calling on me, so I said, "What's a 'tude?"

"Name."

"*'Tude* is a name?" I said.

"Don't get smart with me," he said. I almost couldn't see his eyes now because his eyebrows were in the way. "Tell me your name or you're doing laps."

"Ginger Hollingberry," I said. Well, yelled. My brother also told me I sounded like a bullhorn when I got all worked up.

Coach lifted his chin again, this time at everybody. "Someone tell Hollingberry what a 'tude is."

"I will," Tori said, and turned to me while Kylie's friends groaned with their eyes. "It's short for 'attitude,' and it means when you, you know, pull an attitude."

"Oh," I said. "I don't have one."

Coach Zabriski glared me down until I was sure I was shrinking like Alice in Wonderland, and then he said, "I'm not wasting any more time on this. All right, people, listen up."

Great. I was a waste of time. I now knew what was so bad about Coach Zabriski.

It got worse. He went on and on (and did I mention on?) about the obstacle course behind him—bars and tunnels and ropes and things you had to jump over and, the worst part, a fake rock wall that reached almost as high as the school. If we were going to pass P.E., we had to be able to do it all, including climb to the top of that wall . . . and down. I started hoping for some disease that would last until the grading period was over.

I looked at the Tribelet to see how they were taking this. Ophelia was rebraiding her hair, and I knew in about fifteen seconds, she'd be chewing on the end of it. Winnie was looking pale as a bowl of Cream of Wheat. Tori had her hands shoved into her sweatshirt pockets so that Einstein's face was all long and weird and you couldn't read $E = mc^2$ anymore. Mitch was the only one who didn't act like we were about to be eaten by Orcs, but, then again, nothing scared Mitch. I decided to copy Tori and stuck my hands in my jeans pockets.

"You'll be in four teams," Coach went on some more, shouting like we were downtown instead of standing right in front of him. "Two boys' teams, two girls'."

"Thank you," Winnie whispered.

I nodded. Patrick and Douglas and Andrew (the BBAs) had all signed the Code, but it was hard for them to follow it since they were just naturally obnoxious. As in, probably born that way.

"Don't get your gym shorts in a wad, people," Coach said. "I've already picked the team captains." He glanced down at the clipboard Mrs. Zabriski handed him. "Patrick O'Conner, Fen Wiley, Kylie Steppe, and Tori Taylor."

I stifled a woo-hoo. Tori would pick me for her team. I'd lost count of how many times I hadn't been chosen in the twelve schools I'd been in since first grade. I could get dry mouth just thinking about it.

Coach separated the four team captains. Some people started waving their hands down in front of them at Tori or Kylie or one of the boys—especially the four soccer girls who were their own group, and Evelyn and Shelby, who didn't really have a group they hung out with. Shelby used to be one of "Those Girls," which is what I called Kylie and them in my head. Until a week ago, we referred to them as the Wolf Pack, but that didn't seem right after we came up with the Code.

Coach barked, "Relax!" As if *that* was gonna make anybody calm down. "The team captains aren't picking you. You're picking *them*."

We all just looked at him. I had to consciously close my mouth because it kind of fell open on its own when I was, like, flabbergasted.

"So, go!" he said.

We did. People ran and banged into each other and flattened themselves into lines behind the captains like we were trying to get on lifeboats or something.

I got right in back of Tori with the rest of the Tribelet. No big surprise there. But I did have to shut my mouth again when Evelyn and Shelby and Brittney and Josie and Quinby and Ciara all crowded in behind us. Tori had eleven people on her team.

Kylie? She had four, counting herself: Riannon, her first officer who passed down Kylie's commands; Heidi, who collected information for Kylie for her to use against people; and Izzy, who was the messenger. When you saw her coming your way, you knew it was bad news.

The boys were still shoving and pulling at each other as Coach Zabriski stomped over to the girls. I noticed his legs were short but beefy, like those diagrams of cuts of meat. His were big ol' roasts.

"All right, let's even this up!" he said.

I looked over at Kylie's puny line, and in my head, I whispered, *Somebody please volunteer to go over there before he starts plucking us out.* Memories of my first weeks at Gold Country attacked me, and I totally wanted to retreat to the bathroom. And maybe throw up.

"Iann," Coach said to Mitch, jabbing a stubby finger at her, "move to Steppe's line. And you two." He stabbed the finger at Brittney and Josie. "Go!"

Ophelia and Winnie both watched Mitch change teams like they were never going to see her again.

"It's okay," Tori whispered to us. "Mitch can handle it."

I felt a little better, but only because when Tori said something was going to work out, it usually did. She was all brainy and serious about science, but with anything that had to do with the Code, she was the strongest of us in being against bullying so we could maybe . . . enjoy school. In the twelve I'd been to, this was the first one where I thought that could actually happen.

Kylie (on the other hand) did not look like she felt better. At all. While Coach was counting for about the third time, she swung that hairdo that seemed like it talked and she looked straight at Tori. Her eyes went down into such tight lines I could hardly see the color in them, and if her lip had folded up any farther, she would have sucked it up her nose when she breathed. That was Kylie body language for: *I am not happy. And if* I'm *not happy,* NOBODY *is going to be happy.*

"Threatening Looks" was Number Two on the Code of things we pledged not to do to each other. I pulled my set of "What to Do" cards out of the back pocket of my jeans and flipped through them. Even after only a couple of weeks, they were gray around the edges, and the corners looked like the ears on the border collie that lived across the street. It was still hard for me to know what to do to help other people the way the Tribelet stood up for me.

But Tori didn't exactly need my help. She just looked away from Kylie. Okay. I stuffed the cards back into my pocket and turned my face away too. Which was a good thing, because I was having trouble not smiling as it hit me: the reason Kylie was all prune-faced was because Tori was now more popular than she was.

Kylie had always been what Lydia called the "Queen Bee." Lydia was the grown-up who helped us form our Tribelet and declare war on bullying and come up with the Code for our whole grade. She was going to be glad to hear that the other girls were getting that Kylie wasn't the bee to follow. If Lydia ever came back.

"Aren't you going inside?" somebody said.

I guess I was deeper into that daydream than I thought because I jumped and looked around. Everybody else was headed for the locker room door, which Mrs. Zabriski was holding open. Everybody except me, because I'd been standing there daydreaming like a dork, and Heidi, because . . . well, I had no idea why she was there, but whatever it was, it couldn't be good. My mouth went dry again.

"Oh," I said, because I could never think of anything to say to any of Those Girls.

I twisted toward the building, but Heidi's nose, which was so small it was hardly there, wrinkled as she smiled. The sun gleamed on the (new) blond streaks in the almost-like-Kylie's bob, and she looped her arm through mine the way characters did in books. "Kylie wants you to come be with us."

"It's the middle of class."

"Coach gave us free time in the locker room, silly," she said, giving me the nose-wrinkling smile again. "Pick a locker and then come be with us."

Voices in my head screamed, *Get out of here NOW!* But Heidi held on to me all the way into the girls' locker room, chatty-chat-chatting away about how Kylie brought her makeup kit and she was going to show us how to use eye shadow. She let go finally and said, "We're over there when you're done."

I didn't even look to see where "over there" was. I charged straight for my Tribelet, who were already lined up on a bench between two rows of lockers.

"We saved one for you, Ginger," Winnie said. She pointed to an open metal door.

"What do I do?" I said.

Mitch looked up at me and shook her spiky head. "You gotta pay attention when Coach is talking or you're gonna be puppy chow."

I turned helplessly to Tori, who said, "Bring a lock for it. For now, you just have to put a piece of paper in there with your name on it."

"I'm doing yours," Ophelia said, head bowed over a pad and markers, braid swinging. "I'm doing all of ours."

"And then we're going to work on those poems for English." Tori shuddered like she was about to eat a cockroach. I felt kind of the same way. I liked writing poems, but the assignment was to compose a sonnet about your best quality. I wasn't sure I had one.

"I started mine," Ophelia said.

She flipped her braid over her shoulder and cleared her throat and arranged her hand in the air until Tori said, "Jeepers, Phee. Tell it, already."

Winnie giggled. It sounded the same as a little silver bell, and I liked it.

"Okay, I'm ready," Ophelia said.

Of course she had to clear her throat one more time. I was about to ask her if she wanted a cough drop.

Finally, Ophelia started in. "I woke from my sleep—"

I didn't hear the rest because somebody grabbed my sleeve and pulled me out of our row of lockers. That somebody was Izzy, and her round cheeks were bright red, which meant she had news. Not good. She wasn't as gentle as Heidi as she hauled me around the end of the lockers, and all I could see as she dragged me were the Tribelet's eyes bulging.

In the next row, Those Girls were all posed around Kylie. They each wore the exact same expression—the way starved-skinny models did in magazines. It was like the more the clothes cost, the unhappier they looked. The models in the Kmart ads always seemed like they were about to say, "Woo-hoo!" even though their outfits were cheap. I should be super-ecstatic because my jeans and sweatshirts mostly came from Goodwill.

But when Izzy pulled me into the picture, Kylie looked up and actually smiled as she patted the bench beside her. Her deep dimples even showed like little finger-pokes into whipped cream.

"Come sit by me," she said.

"Why?" I said.

Riannon rolled her green eyes—like, way up into her head—and Heidi covered her mouth with her hand (although I heard her snort). Izzy gave me a shove toward Kylie.

"Don't be rough with her," Kylie said to her. To me she said, "I know I haven't been that nice to you in the past."

Like at all.

"And since that whole Code thing and all, I thought I should . . . be nicer."

I *didn't* remind Kylie that she was the only person in the whole sixth grade who hadn't *signed* the Code. I *did* remember to close my mouth.

"I don't know what Vic*tor*ia has told you," Kylie said, (she was talking about Tori), "but I'm not some monster."

"She never called you a monster," I said, although *I'd* sure wanted to—like a hundred times.

But Kylie was still smiling at me. She and Those Girls had been suspended for five days, and, as they had just found out, they'd lost their place as the popular ones while they were gone. So maybe . . . that might have changed them some? If I was going to follow the Code, shouldn't I sit down and give them a chance?

So I took a seat on the bench next to Kylie. On the other side of her, Heidi was holding a big, plastic, pink, polka-dot, zippered thing that opened out flat and held more makeup than they had at Raley's. Not that I knew anything about cosmetics, but yikes!

"We're doing makeovers," Kylie said.

"And we thought you could use one," Riannon said.

Heidi didn't even try to smother her snort that time.

Kylie glared at them before she smiled at me again with her perfect teeth showing. "I just thought it would be fun for you."

Without waiting for me to say, "Sure," or "No way!" she pushed my hair back with a headband and went after my cheeks with a big soft brush that had pink powder on it.

"This will give you cheekbones," she said.

Or make me look like Ronald McDonald. Yeah, it was hard to believe she'd changed *that* much.

Kylie handed the brush to Riannon and held out her palm until Heidi put a mascara wand into it. It was reminding me of an operating room on TV.

"Be really still," Kylie said to me.

Still? I was suddenly paralyzed.

"You actually look sort of good," Heidi said when Kylie was finished with my eyelashes. I continued to hold my breath.

Kylie held up three tubes. "What color lip gloss do you want?"

"Go with the Chocolate Shakespeare," Riannon said.

"Does it taste like chocolate?" I couldn't help asking.

"Of course." Kylie slathered some on me like she did it all the time. Which, come to think of it, she did. Those girls were always gooping up their lips. I licked mine. It did taste kind of like a Hershey's kiss.

"Now, hair," Kylie said.

She stood up, brush in hand, got behind me, and took off the headband. I waited for her to yank me bald-headed, but the strokes were soft. Nobody had brushed my hair for me since I was six.

"We don't even know that much about you," Kylie said. "Right?"

The girls nodded. I looked for eye rolls or lip curls or that thing they did when they were trying—not that hard—not to laugh in my face. But they all looked interested, leaning-in and nodding like they were.

"Like, for example, doesn't your mom ever talk to you about clothes and hair and stuff?"

I felt myself go stiff again. Should I say it? I didn't tell people because they always acted weird around me afterward. But Kylie was being nice. Maybe nice enough.

"I don't have a mom," I said.

"Why?"

"She died when I was in first grade."

Everybody's eyes got bigger. Izzy started looking around like she wanted to escape, as if somebody's mom dying was contagious. Kylie stopped brushing. I wanted to bite my whole tongue off.

"That is so *sad*," she said. "What happened?"

Now *I* wanted to escape. We weren't supposed to talk about it, Jackson and me. I didn't know why, and I'd stopped asking because it made my dad get in a bad mood and my brother go further into his cave.

Kylie came back around to the front of me and straddled the bench. She handed the hairbrush off to Izzy over her shoulder and put her face really close to mine. She was way prettier when she looked all soft like that.

"Is it hard to talk about?" she said.

"No," I said. I actually *wanted* to talk about it, but nobody would. But to Those Girls?

Kylie leaned in even closer. She smelled like strawberries. "Do you *want* to talk about it? I would totally listen."

I knew my eyes were bugging out, and I couldn't help it. Did she, like, read my mind?

"I've had people die in my family too," she said. "I know I'd get it. I could probably even help you."

"She was in a car accident," I blurted out.

"I am *so* sorry," she said. "Were you in the car with her?"

"No."

"So what happened?"

"I don't know that much," I said. "Somebody else was driving and . . . that's all I know. My dad doesn't like to talk about it."

Kylie's blue-and-gold eyes drooped. "That is *sad*. So that's why you don't do the girly thing? Because you lost your mom?"

"I guess so," I said. That and the fact that I wasn't even a little bit pretty, so what was the point? Tori once told me my eyes were like two blueberries, so that might be okay, but other than that, I was short—but not as little as Winnie—and freckly and not skinny like Those Girls (well, except Izzy, who was kind of round). I thought I was sort of smushy.

"Well, look at yourself now," Kylie said.

Riannon stuck a mirror in front of me so I had to look even though I didn't want to because I was sure she had painted me to look like Bozo. But I wasn't that bad. I was pinker. Shinier. Fluffier.

"You should totally do that every day," Heidi said, her blond streaks shining as she tilted her head. "You look so much better."

"And anytime you want to talk to us about your mom, you can," Kylie said.

They nodded like they were one person. I started to nod with them, but in that very moment, I saw it. The fast cut of Heidi's eyes to Riannon's and back just as quick. The red gathering in Izzy's cheeks. The gleam of the gold specks in Kylie's eyes.

I had just been made fun of—again—and I didn't even know how it happened.

Chapter Two

We had tests in second-period social studies (with Mr. Jett, who doubled as the cafeteria monitor and always looked like a Doberman pinscher to me) and third-period math (with Mrs. Collier-Callahan, who was sort of an old shih tzu) and fourth-period science (with Mr. Vasiliev, who we called Mr. V and who was a very cool Labrador retriever). Whenever I wasn't filling in blanks and marking true and false, I was thinking about what I blurted out to Those Girls about my mom.

The whole rest of the day, during lunch and fifth period with Mrs. Fickus (the English teacher/yellow poodle with a Southern accent) and sixth period with Mrs. Bernstein (the Spanish teacher/Chihuahua), I felt funky for the first time in a whole week. You know, like my eyes were all darting around like a squirrel's. And at lunch I couldn't eat my peanut-butter-and-pickle sandwich, so I just tore it into little pieces so it would look like I was eating it.

The Tribelet asked me what was going on.

MITCH: What's *wrong* with you? You're acting weird.

TORI: You okay, Ginge?

WINNIE: Want a cookie?

OPHELIA: Did Kylie do something mean to you? You're
supposed to tell us, you know.

But what I *wasn't* supposed to do was talk about my mom's accident, and now I'd done it, and it was tying my stomach into big knots.

ME: I already opened my big mouth today, so I should keep
it shut now.

THEM: Huh?

∽

On the walk home from school that day, with Jackson trailing behind
me so he could pretend he didn't know me (because a seventh-grade
boy doesn't want to be seen hanging out with his sixth-grade sister),
I didn't do my usual daydreaming about the crooked little yellow
and blue houses built over where gold mines used to be. Instead, I
spent the whole time going over the scene with Those Girls about
eighty-seven times. I decided maybe by being nice to me they were
just trying not to get in any more trouble. Getting suspended for five
days was the biggest thing ever, so it must have shaken something up
in them, right? If that had happened to me, I would curl up in a ball
in the bottom of my closet and never come out.

Okay, maybe I'd come out to eat.

Jackson kept the key to our house because Dad didn't get home
until six and Jackson didn't lose as much stuff as I did. He also got
to use the computer first after school. It was new (because my dad

said things were going better with his business), and we'd both just gotten e-mail, and Jackson, like, lived on it. When he wasn't caved in his room like the creature Gollum playing video games. I called him Sméagol in my head. I liked to think of myself as Frodo from *The Lord of the Rings*.

"How long are you gonna be on there?" I said to him as I pawed through the snack drawer. We were only allowed to eat stuff out of there when Dad wasn't home. He got tired of starting supper and finding out Jackson and I had eaten all the ingredients.

"On where?" Jackson said.

He reached around me and pulled out the granola bar I already had my hand on.

"On the computer."

"I'm not getting on the computer."

"Oh. Why not? You always do. Are you sick?"

I straightened to look at him, a package of cheese crackers in my hand, which I put behind my back so he couldn't grab it. Not that he would actually eat it. He was as tall and skinny as I was shortish and . . . smushy. And while we're on the subject of looks, he didn't get Dad's red hair either. His was all thick and blond and wavy like in the pictures of our mom. He even had her eyelashes that almost looked like false ones. Totally wasted on a boy. So not fair.

"No, I'm not sick," he said. "I just have other stuff to do. What did you get?"

"It's mine," I said. "What other stuff?"

"None-of-your-business stuff."

"Is it about a girl?"

Jackson squinted his blue eyes, which were the only feature we both had, so I guess they were like blueberries too. If you can imagine berries that said, "You are a moron."

"Yeah, it's about a girl," he said. "The chicks are all over me. I'm a total babe magnet. I gotta fend 'em off with a stick."

"No, you don't," I said.

"Then why did you even ask me that?" Jackson put up his hand, kind of the way Dad did when he was done answering my questions. "Never mind. You can have the computer for twenty minutes. And don't mess it up."

I didn't argue with him because, really, I could mess just about anything up. I didn't even take the cheese crackers with me to the little desk Dad had found a place for in the corner of our tiny dining area. That's where the computer was, and next to it was a piece of paper with the list of steps for getting on my e-mail. Dad did that so I wouldn't accidentally erase any of his work stuff. He had his own house remodeling business, which was why we had to move so much. "We go where the work is," he always said. I wished the work hadn't been in a dozen different places.

I had three new e-mails. One was from Tori saying, *If you need to talk, call me.* The second was from Ophelia, and it was, like, two pages long about how I shouldn't be like some Shakespeare thing where a guy kept everything to himself and ended up dying, along with everybody else in the play. I mean, huh?

The third one was from somebody named K4FAIR, and the subject said, *Important for Ginger.*

I clutched the mouse like it might get away and tried to remember what Dad said when he sat Jackson and me down and lectured us about Internet rules. *Don't ever open an e-mail from anybody you don't know* was definitely one of them because right after that Jackson said, "Ginger doesn't know anybody, so that shouldn't be hard." I'd jabbed him with my elbow. He'd pretended like I broke one of his ribs. Dad told us both to get serious. So, yeah, I remembered that rule.

And no, I didn't know K4FAIR. But, then, I didn't know the screen names for every girl in my class—just the Tribelet's. I didn't even know Lydia's.

Wait, could this be from her? She had never e-mailed me before, but she might now. She should be out of rehab after her surgery and maybe she was coming back to work for Tori's dad again and be our mentor and teach the classes at school for people who didn't sign the Code or violated it.

K could stand for Kiriakos, her last name. She was all *about* people being treated fair. And *Important for Ginger* would be just like something she'd put in a subject line. I wiggled the mouse. If it wasn't from her, I'd just close it and delete it. It wasn't going to jump out of the screen and eat my face . . .

I clicked it open. And felt my mouth come open so far it was like my jaws didn't have hinges anymore.

We'll find out the whole story about your mom's accident, Gingerbread. It was totally something bad or your father wouldn't have told you not to talk about it. Or maybe he did and you're not telling US. Which is stupid because who lies to us and thinks she can get away with it? We think we know, and it is NOT GOOD. We'll find out for sure.

But don't worry. When we do, we won't spread this all over the entire school. We won't tell anybody IF (and you better pay attention here, which you're not very good at doing) you stop hanging out with Tori Taylor and Winnie George and Ophelia Smith and Michelle Iann. Your little group. But if you keep being with them, EVERYBODY will know how your mother died. And we mean EVERYBODY.

HINT: It has to do with what everybody knows about getting in a car with someone who shouldn't be driving.

We'll be watching you, so don't try anything sneaky. Not that you're smart enough to.

I knew my face was going blotchy, but I put my hands up anyway to feel the hot spots on my neck and my cheeks and the top of my forehead where the hair started. My face was still all goopy with their makeup, and I scrubbed at it with my fingers. I really thought they'd changed. Was I stupid or what?

I looked at the red stuff on my fingertips. That wasn't really the question right now. The question was: What was I supposed to *do*? What did Dad say? Something like, *If you get any e-mail that's dirty or crude, delete it right away.*

What about something that was totally made up? My mom didn't do anything she wasn't supposed to. She would never do that to us. Right? I mean, *right*? The knots in my stomach got tighter. I didn't lie to Those Girls when I told them I didn't know what exactly happened, so how were *they* going to find out?

Or what about an e-mail that tried to cut me off from the only friends I had ever had since kindergarten? The *only* friends.

I stared at the screen until it got blurry. Should I delete it like it never happened? Or should I tell somebody? But who? Lydia? I didn't know how to get in touch with her. Tori or Mitch? But wouldn't they say I was nuts to ever have told Those Girls anything, ever? Should I tell Dad about it maybe?

"Where are my children?"

I went into a spasm in the chair. I thought his name and he showed up? Really?

"Ginger! Jackson! Yo!"

Dad's voice coming across the living room was jolly, like somebody playing Santa. He never sounded that happy. I closed my eyes and tried to imagine myself saying, "Let me show you something that's going to put you in the blackest mood ever." I couldn't do it. Just as he got to the dining area, I pushed the cursor up to *delete* and clicked the mouse. The e-mail went away seconds before Dad's big freckled hand squeezed my shoulder and let go.

"Why are you home so early?" I said too loud.

"Finished the job. Thought I'd take you kids to that hot dog place."

"Hot Dog Heaven?" Jackson said on his way down the hall. "Sweet."

"Figured we'd go now, before it gets crowded."

Any other time I would have already had my shoes half on and charged to the front door. We didn't go out to eat that often, and Hot Dog Heaven might not sound like that big of a deal, but they made the best dogs I ever, ever had, and all of them were named after actual breeds—like The German Shepherd (which came with sauerkraut). Plus, they had a bajillion different kinds of chips. Besides all that, when did Dad ever come home from work all cheerful like a father on a sitcom? Yeah, any other time, that would have made me babble stuff until Jackson told me I sounded like I'd just sucked on a helium balloon.

But this wasn't any other time.

All the way to the strip mall I sat in the back of Dad's work van, where he'd installed a seat so I could be behind and between him and Jackson, and I thought about the e-mail. I'd only read it once, but it was burned into my brain. I was pretty sure it would totally combust if I didn't tell somebody.

Twice I opened my mouth to do it. Both times something stopped me.

The first time it was Dad, telling Jackson he'd pay him to clean out the brush in the back of the yard that the landlord hadn't taken care of. It was getting to be nicer weather, Dad said, and we needed to get a little grill and start barbecuing out there. Dad said that. Dad never planned anything for us past the next week. But Dad said that.

The second time it was Jackson. He opened the passenger side

window and leaned his pointy elbow out and told Dad he was thinking about joining this club at school where everybody designed their
own comic books. Jackson had spent most of his time in his room
since he was ten years old, when it kind of hit him that Mom was
never coming back. He wore all black and had more conversations
with his video games than he did with Dad and me. Especially me.
But here he was saying he wanted to join something.

I put my hand on my chin and pushed my mouth closed. If I told
them about this—in fact, if they found out any way at all—they would
both go back into those sad, dark places they stayed in all the time,
and I would be alone again.

I pressed myself into the seat and squeezed my eyes shut. I was
going to be alone anyway, because the only way to make sure they
didn't find out was not to be friends with . . .

I couldn't even think it.

When we'd ordered our dogs and picked out our chips and got to
our usual orange plastic booth, Dad said he had to go wash his hands,
which left me with Jackson. I pulled a napkin out of the dispenser
and started turning it into confetti.

"I thought Dad was gonna tell us we were moving again," Jackson said.

"Are you talking to me?" I said.

Jackson looked around the booth. "You see anybody else here?"

I shook my head and tore off more pieces.

"He always takes us out to eat when he has to tell us we're moving."

"He does?"

"Yeah."

"Why?"

"Because we're not gonna make a scene about it in public."
Jackson squinted the blueberries again. "Well, at least I'm not."

"I don't do that," I said, although the lady in the next booth looked
over at me like I was talking too loud.

"No, Freak Show." Jackson pointed to the tabletop. "You just tear stuff up. It looks like it snowed over here. What's up with that?"

"Clear the deck," Dad said.

He was coming toward us with a tray. I swiped the "snow" into my lap. Then I started shredding the bun Dad put in front of me.

"Got some good news for you kids."

"We're not moving," Jackson said.

I could tell Dad was disappointed because the freckles around his mouth sort of sagged.

"What makes you think that?" he said.

Jackson lifted his bony shoulders to his ears. "You want to clean up the yard and cook out there. And you didn't tell me not to count on joining the comic book club." He shrugged again. "It adds up."

"Guess I ruined my own surprise." Dad's lips did that spread-out-go-back-in thing, which was as much of a smile as he ever seemed to be able to get going. "I got another job here in Grass Valley . . . a remodel on an old house on Church Street."

"Where the rich people live," Jackson said.

"These people are. The job'll take at least six or seven months. Thought you'd like that. You two seem happier here than you have anyplace else."

I sucked my lips in so I wouldn't say, "Until today."

"It's okay here," my brother said, which was Jacksonese for, *I would do a cartwheel right now if it wouldn't make me look like a dweeb.*

Dad turned his stormy gray-blue eyes to me, and I tried to do what Ophelia would do: my best acting job.

"Yay," I said. I smiled and tried to do a happy wiggle in the seat, which sent my napkin snow all over the floor.

But Dad's freckles sagged a little more.

"I'm happy, really," I said. I looked at Jackson. "I'm just trying not to make a scene."

Dad play-smacked Jackson on the back of the head, and his eyes smiled some as he chewed a big hunk of The German Shepherd.

It would be okay, then, until I could get home and try to figure this out.

When we pulled into the driveway, I tried not to flee from the van like I was being chased by a pack of rottweilers or skid on the rug in the hallway running for my room, but it seemed like the click of the lock on my bedroom door echoed out into the rest of the house, the way it does in prison movies. If either Dad or Jackson noticed, they didn't come around asking. For once, that was a good thing.

I sank onto the pile of orange and red floor pillows I'd talked Dad into buying for me on our last thrift store run—I called it my Hobbit Seat—and leaned against the wall under the front window. The border collie across the street was barking, probably because the sun was setting or a pine needle fell, but I blocked him out. I tried to block everything out, the way I usually could in my room. It was my Rivendell.

That was the peaceful land where the Elves live in *The Lord of the Rings*, which I knew more about than I did just about anything. You didn't have to be in my room for more than, like, seven seconds to figure that out.

Dad had built me bookshelves that covered the one wall that didn't have the headboard on the bed, the closet, or the window to interrupt it. I had it filled with books I loved, but especially everything Tolkien and Hobbits and Gandalf. Jackson and I didn't get presents except for our birthdays and Christmas, and all I ever asked for were more books and posters and DVDs about all of it. A map of Middle Earth hung over my bed, and I'd taped a poster of Gandalf from the movie on my closest door. Under the picture it said, *All those who wander are not lost.*

I read and watched over and over, and usually that took me into a world where the bullies were conquered and the fighters against bullying always won. There I could be Frodo, the unlikely choice to save the world from evil. It almost always helped.

But not that night. So I crawled from my Hobbit Seat to the bed, where I stuck my hand between the mattress and the box spring and pulled out a thin binder. It was decorated with stickers of Hobbits and Aragorn and Legolas—what else *was* there to decorate with?—but the inside wasn't dedicated to *The Lord of the Rings*. It was where I kept a list that nobody knew about. Not even my Tribelet.

A knot tied itself in my stomach, but I tried to ignore it as I studied the list.

Things Nobody Knows About Me

1. I am a Tolkien freak.
2. I sometimes act out scenes from *The Lord of the Rings* when I'm by myself.
3. I love costumes even though I don't have any.
4. I am writing my own fantasy novel in my head.
5. I want to be a professional writer someday.
6. I'm smarter than I act like I am.
7. My mom was killed in a car accident.
8. I don't know why, and I'm mad at God.

The first six things on the list were there because I used to try to tell people that stuff about myself and they looked at me like *I* was the creature Gollum. After that, they used it to make fun of me.

Two schools ago, a group of Those Girls brought me a cape so I could dress up like Gandalf, but when I put it on, it had clumps of cat fur in it big as hamsters, and I had to walk around the rest of the day with hair all over me and people sneezing every time they looked at me. None of the teachers did anything about it.

That was when I made my list, and after that I never talked about the things on it to anybody. Even the Tribelet. They would never try to make me look like a freak because I liked Tolkien, so maybe I'd tell them someday. But not yet.

I ran my finger down to Number Seven. That was on there because, like I've said, I just wasn't allowed to talk about my mom's accident. Dad never said, "Don't!" but it made him go into a deep hole, and everything was so much harder when he was down there. That wasn't the only reason either.

The other reason was one of those things I wasn't supposed to hear but I did. It was only about a year after my mom died, so I was seven. We were still living in Santa Clara in our house, the one we got when Mom got her nurse practitioner license and a new job. Before she died, it was all sunshiny and clean and smelled like lemons all the time, but after the accident, Dad kept the curtains closed and my tennis shoes stuck to the kitchen floor and the whole place smelled like dirty socks and milk that went bad.

That day I was behind the couch, reading *The Lion, the Witch, and the Wardrobe* because I didn't have a Hobbit Seat yet (because I didn't *know* about the Hobbits yet), and my grandma came over, my mom's mom. She stormed all around the living room, pushing the curtains open and telling my dad he better "come out of it" or she was going to take Jackson and me to live with her.

Dad said, "You can't do that. They're my kids. They're all I have."

Grandma said, in that voice that reminded me of tight wire, "Then climb out of this black hole you're in and start taking care of them. Or I will file for custody, Pete. I will."

My stomach tied itself into a knot now, just like it did then. Ever since that day, I opened curtains and washed dishes and made good grades and did everything I could so my dad wouldn't sink into the blackness and Grandma wouldn't come in with her wire voice and take us away. Most important of all, I tried not to talk about the accident.

But today, I might have messed it up.

I got out my purple Sharpie and crossed out: *My mom was killed in a car accident.* Now somebody did know about that. Somebody who wanted to twist it and make it ugly.

That was my own fault. Maybe I *was* just that Gingerbread Girl who deserved to get bullied.

"Ginger!" Dad called from the dining room. Jackson never said *he* had a bullhorn voice, but he kind of did. "Phone!"

Who is it? I wanted to call back. *If she says her name is Kylie, would you tell her I dried up and blew away? Please?*

But Dad didn't know much about the way I got treated when we first moved to Grass Valley. I considered that as I trudged down the hall. He couldn't leave work and go to the parents' meeting in our principal Mrs. Yeats's office that everybody else's moms or dads had gone to the day it all came out. He'd only read the letter she sent out about the Code and how the school was cracking down on meanness. If I told him now that the girl on the phone was a bully, he would probably just say, "So ignore her."

If I could, wouldn't I have done it already?

But it wasn't Kylie's voice on the other end of the line. It was Tori, and she sounded excited. As in, she talked fast and her sentences all had exclamation points at the ends.

"Lydia's back!" she said.

"At your house?" I said.

"Well, at her apartment, but she's back working for my dad! And guess what?"

"Wh—"

"She wants to meet with the Tribelet, here, after school tomorrow. Can you ask your dad if you can come?"

Dad was sitting three feet from me, blinking at the computer screen. My heart went into hyper speed as I peered over his shoulder, but he was reading some article about shutters or something. I did delete that e-mail, right? It was gone, yes?

"Can you?" Tori said in my ear.

Could I?

We won't tell anybody IF . . . you stop hanging out with Tori Taylor and Winnie George and Ophelia Smith and Michelle Iann. Your little group.

Was having a Tribelet meeting considered "hanging out"?

But if you keep being with them, EVERYBODY will know how your mother died.

I couldn't be with them at school. I couldn't. But what if I was with them someplace where Kylie couldn't see? And she didn't say anything about Lydia. Lydia—the one person who might be able to help me.

"Are you okay, Ginge?" Tori said.

Her voice was so nice, the knot that was my stomach almost untied and let me cry. I had to take a chance or I really would dry up and blow away.

"I'll ask my dad," I said.

And for the first time since the locker room, I felt a tiny flicker of hope.

Chapter Three

The first words out of my mouth the next morning—before the sun even peeked through the Grass Valley evergreens—were, "I want you to SHUT UP!"

The border collie across the street was carrying on like a band of robbers was carting away his entire house. Were the people who lived over there deaf?

I pulled my pillow over my head, but his high-pitched yipping came right through the down feathers. If they weren't going to tell him to knock it off, I was. I pretty much fell out of bed—because I was all tied up in the covers—and stomped to the window. Then I yanked it up and opened my mouth to yell, "QUIET!!!"

But the word stuck in my throat. All I could do was stare, mouth hanging all the way open. Even though I was still halfway between sleeping and being awake, I knew what I was looking at.

The two big trees in our front yard were draped and looped and wrapped in so much toilet paper, I couldn't even *see* the dog across the street. To make it even worse, a thin drizzle of rain was slowly soaking it so that it all sagged and stuck and made our entire front yard look like it was being flushed down the john.

My stomach grabbed itself. It grabbed even harder when I heard Dad open the front door.

"What the Sam Hill?" he said.

I shut the window and leaped for the bed. Maybe if I went back to sleep and woke up again I'd find out this was just one of my nightmares. But a very real Dad knocked on my door.

"You awake?"

"Huh?" I said.

"Look out front. Surprise for you."

There was kind of a chuckle in his voice. He thought this was *funny*?

I sat up and gave it a few seconds and said, "Yikes."

"Somebody likes you."

Likes me? Was he serious?

"Who likes Ginger?" I heard Jackson say in that thick way he talked when he wasn't awake yet. Like, until about noon. "This I gotta see."

Dad rapped on my door again, so I said, "Come in," which they both did. Jackson followed Dad's point to the window and stood there with his back to me.

"We all did that to our friends when I was a kid," Dad said. He sounded like he was proud.

"It doesn't mean . . ." I started to say.

But Jackson whipped his head around and stared the words off my lips. The blueberry eyes said, *Upset Dad and I will end you.*

Dad did the almost-smile thing and gave my toes a quick squeeze through the bedspread. "Enjoy it for now. Clean it up when you get home today. Gotta get ready for work."

When he'd left the room, Jackson leaned his hands on the bottom of my bed. "This is what you get for being all into that anti-bullying thing. Which means *you* can clean it up." He turned toward the door and then looked back at me, eyes in blue slits. "Don't tell Dad what this is really about. He thinks we're totally good right now."

Like he actually had to tell me that. Or like Dad had to tell me to clean it up. I wasn't waiting for after school—I was going for it right now.

I pulled one of Dad's old sweatshirts on over my pajamas, and jammed my feet into my sneakers, and went out the front door. My foot immediately slipped, and I had to grab onto the wobbly railing around our tiny front porch to keep from falling down the steps. When I looked to see what I'd stepped in, I almost barfed.

Dog poop. A big pile of it. And we didn't have a dog.

Gagging, I hopped on my clean foot down the steps and grabbed some big wet leaves. I rubbed the poopy shoe on another pile of leaves on the ground and used the handful to get the worst of it off the porch. That was when something caught my eye in the shrub beside the steps. Something pink.

With polka dots.

Even as I reached for it, I already knew it was Kylie's makeup case. It was zipped up and bulging, but I didn't open it. There was probably a snake in there or something. Why else would she bring it to a TP-ing?

Unless it accidentally dropped out of her bag.

Across the street, the dog was absolutely going crazy, and Jackson came to the door.

"Would you come in so he'll shut up?" His face twisted as he looked at me. "Are you out there in your *pajamas*? That's it. I'm changing my last name."

I would've come back with something, but I wanted him to go inside before he smelled the poop. He shook his head like I was some kind of math problem he couldn't solve and went back in the house.

I hosed off the front porch, stuck the makeup kit under my shirt, and considered pretending I had appendicitis. Except I'd used that excuse three times already.

After the bullying of me had stopped—eight days ago—I'd started to like walking to school. Grass Valley wasn't like any other town we ever lived in in California because it was sort of old-timey, like back in the Gold Rush days (which Tori knew all about because her father was a history person, and so was Lydia). I could close my eyes and imagine wearing a dress down to my ankles and being rich because my father struck gold. Plus, Grass Valley had its own smell, probably from the pine trees everywhere and because there was hardly any pollution. I could breathe really deep as I walked up and down the hills and not start wheezing and having my eyes turn red from allergies, which made me look like a frog. Or at least that was what I'd been told. More than once.

But that day on the way to school, with my sweatshirt hood up to keep the drizzle from turning my hair into carrot shreds, I couldn't think about anything but what to do once I got there.

I couldn't just walk up to Kylie and cry and say, "Why did you put poop on my porch?" I used to do stuff like that, and it only made things worse. *Save the Tears* was one of the cards in my pocket.

But if I pretended it didn't happen, Those Girls would do something worse. When grown-ups said, "Just ignore it when someone picks on you," they obviously had never been bullied in their life.

I patted the pocket with the cards in it. I didn't pull any out because they'd get wet, and besides, I knew what they all said anyway.

- SAVE THE TEARS. *Don't let the bully see that she's getting to you.*
- BABY STEPS. *Do one small thing to end bullying because you can't do everything at once.*

- SAFE IN A GROUP. *Don't make a victim face a bunch of bullies by herself.*
- WALK IT, GIRL. *Help each other go where you want to go without being harassed.*
- REPORT ALERT. *Tell a grown-up if the bullying gets out of control.*
- GOLD THUMB. *Do for other people what you want them to do for you.*

That was the hardest one in the whole stack to follow. I didn't really *want* to do anything for Those Girls. But Lydia had taught us that was the whole point. It wasn't about what we wanted to do. It was about what was right to do. And the only thing right I could think of was to give Kylie's makeup kit back to her.

The rain was coming down like bullets by the time I got to school. Instead of going to the top of the stairs by the sixth-grade lockers to hang out with my Tribelet, like I always did before first period, I went straight to the locker room. I'd rather change into my P.E. clothes by myself anyway. Nobody else's body was as smushy as mine.

I was in my sweatpants and T-shirt when Tori got there.

"Ginge!" she said. "Where were you?"

"Here," I said.

She blinked her little brown eyes at me. It was like they belonged to a very smart bird. "Did you ask your dad?"

"About what?"

"About coming to my house after school?"

"Oh. Yeah. He said yes."

"Cool," she said, but she kept looking at me. I was never glad to hear Mrs. Zabriski before that moment when she yelled into the locker room.

"Meet in the gym, not outside. And let's get a move on."

Tori gave me one more bird look and, as the rest of the Tribelet trailed in, she turned to change her clothes. My mind was already on to the next thing. If we were meeting in the gym for roll call, that was my perfect chance. I got the pink zipper case out of my locker and once again tucked it under my sweatshirt.

Kylie and Those Girls were in their usual knot, four rows up in the bleachers. I started to climb up there, but Mitch grabbed my sweatshirt sleeve and tugged me back.

"You mad at me?" she said into my ear.

"No!" I said.

"You're acting like it." She stuck her nose near her armpit. "Do I smell?"

"No. I just gotta do something. I'll be right back."

I wasn't going to be right back, of course. The words in the e-mail were shouting in my *other* ear.

I was pretty sure Kylie and Those Girls didn't see me talking to Mitch because they were still facing each other and whispering and copying everything Kylie did. If she tilted her head, they tilted theirs. If she fluffed out her hair, they fluffed out theirs. I bet if she'd picked her nose, they would have poked their fingers in their nostrils too.

Mrs. Zabriski was just coming into the gym, so I still had time before she started attendance and announcements. Besides that, Coach came in from the other direction and they stopped to talk. More time.

I climbed over the first three levels of bleachers and then headed sideways down the row they were all crowded onto. It was hard going with the makeup kit under my shirt, so I was probably making a spectacle of myself. You know, tripping once, almost losing my balance twice. By the time I got to their spot, all four of them were looking at me. I knew the blotches were all over my face and neck like splashes of fuchsia paint, but that was okay. This was all about the *Gold Thumb*.

Kylie nudged Riannon, who poked Heidi, who said in her stuffy-nosed voice, "We're not doing makeovers today."

Could that have been more perfect? For once in my life, I knew exactly what should come out of my mouth.

"I know," I said, "because you don't have this." I pulled the makeup kit from under my shirt.

Kylie's eyes bulged. "Give me that!" she said and tried to grab it from me.

My twelve years being Jackson's sister weren't wasted on me. I pulled it out of her reach and said, "I think you dropped it when you were doing your thing—"

"I don't even know what you're talking about." Kylie's voice went up, and then she lowered it. She splashed her hair. "And even if I did, anything that happens off the school grounds isn't the school's business."

Was that just my lucky day or what? I tried not to smile too goofy. "How did you know I was talking about something that happened off school grounds?"

I thought Kylie's blue and gold eyes were going to pop out of her head. All of Those Girls turned to statues, except Kylie herself who quickly pulled her eyeballs back in and folded her arms and said, "Isn't making a false accusation against your little Code?"

I started to say, "I'm not accusing you—"

But the moment I opened my mouth, she snapped out her hand, quick as a frog's tongue, and tried to snatch the makeup kit again. I didn't know why I hung on to it. Maybe because I felt my luck running out. Or maybe because my whole plan was to hand it over to her myself.

Whatever the reason, I snatched it back. Kylie made another grab for it and caught the big pink zipper pull. I yanked the kit toward me. She pulled it toward *her*, and in the process of all that, the bag opened and something flew out like it had been stuffed in there so long it couldn't wait to escape.

It was something pink, and it sailed over the heads of the kids in the next row down and came to rest in the middle of the BBAs. There was a shocked silence, like everybody was waiting for a bomb to explode, and then Patrick waved it over his head and shouted, "Hey, this isn't mine!"

Of course it wasn't. It was a bright pink bra. Tiny and lacy. And padded.

The silence erupted into chaos. I sat down hard on the bleacher bench. Kylie pushed Izzy, who fell all over herself to get to Patrick to grab the bra from him—well, from Douglas, who now had it—oh, wait, from Andrew, who was about to shoot it out across the gym floor like a slingshot when Coach Zabriski blew his whistle and brought the whole thing to a hold-your-breath stop.

Coach held out his palm for the bra, but the moment Andrew started to give it to him, Coach retracted his hand and Mrs. Zabriski took the thing. She stuck it in the pocket of her workout jacket and waved a yellow piece of paper over her head.

"Do you know what this is?" she shouted at us.

Like anybody was even going to try to answer that question. I couldn't have if she'd called on me. I was considering dropping under the bleachers.

"This is an announcement we just got this morning. It says any sixth-grader who violates the Code for"—she looked closer at the paper—"disrespecting the whatever is to be sent to a special class—*during lunch*—every Monday and Thursday until . . ." She studied the paper again. "Until Ms. Ki-ri-a-kos is satisfied with how you treat people."

I knew that was Lydia she was talking about, even though Mrs. Zabriski pronounced her name wrong. Relief started to flood over me.

"It's also for anybody who didn't sign the Code." Mrs. Zabriski swept her hard little gaze over the class, but she didn't say anything. She didn't have to. Everybody knew that meant Kylie.

I was still confused, though, because, until that moment, Mrs. Zabriski never acted like she cared anything about our anti-bullying campaign, and now she was upholding it. Yikes, this meant all of Those Girls might end up in Lydia's class with Kylie. Did I finally do something right?

"Hollingberry!"

I jerked and looked down at her.

"Did you get that? You. Monday at lunch. Report to the conference room in the library."

Me? *Me?*

"You deliberately embarrassed somebody, and I'm not having it. Especially from someone who supposedly helped write this 'Code.'"

Coach stuck his whistle in his mouth and blew until you could see his scalp turning red. "In your teams for timed sprints! Let's move it!"

I moved, and so did my mind. I had no problem spending lunch with Lydia. I *wanted* to talk to her. But with *Kylie* there? And not only that, but why was *I* the one being accused of being a bully? I was the victim. Again.

But as I lined up with Tori down on the gym floor and Winnie whimpered and Ophelia chewed her braid and Mitch looked over at me from Kylie's line like *What were you THINKING?* I decided the worst part was that I made the Code look bad.

Like always, when I tried to do something good, it turned out so stupid.

So it didn't even matter that Kylie was going to do something to me during these timed sprints, whatever *they* were, to get back at me for what just happened. She couldn't make things any worse.

Coach tooted that whistle again, so shrill it went through my fillings, and yelled, "Hollingberry!"

"She's not even doing anything," Ophelia muttered between clenched teeth.

"Save the Tears, Ginger," Tori whispered.

I pretended not to hear them because Kylie was standing next to Coach and Mrs. Zabriski, watching me and talking to them (with her hair) at the same time. All I could do was try not to cry, just like Tori said. Later I could. But not in front of the bully.

"Steppe's trying to be the bigger person," Mrs. Z was saying to her husband when I got to them.

"That's exactly right," Kylie said.

Better person than what? A gorilla?

"Okay," Coach said, "but then I'm done with the girl drama." He barely looked at me. "You're on Steppe's team now."

I almost said no to a teacher for the first time in my life. Tears blurred my eyes as I looked back at the line behind Riannon.

Izzy. Heidi. All looking at me like I was an insect. The only thing that made me blink the tears away was Mitch. She nodded her spiky head just enough to keep me from having a meltdown right there in front of everyone.

Coach put his whistle to his lips, and I covered my ears, but I still heard Kylie whisper to Mrs. Zabriski, "Ginger only acts that way because Tori Taylor intimidates her."

I didn't look to see if Mrs. Zabriski nodded. I just knew she did.

Chapter Four

Coach Zabriski didn't pay any more attention to me during P.E. because he was all over Tori the whole period. She wasn't running fast enough. She wasn't encouraging her team enough. She was showing a 'tude.

It was all my fault—again—and I had to do something about it.

I stayed away from my Tribelet second, third, and fourth periods because Kylie watched me like she had lasers for eyes. But I knew that right after fourth, Those Girls always went to the bathroom to fluff and gloss before lunch—why, I could never figure out—and I would have a chance to at least apologize to Tori. I had it all rehearsed in my head.

ME: I should have just given the kit back to Kylie without saying anything. I made things awful, and I hope you forgive me.

TORI: Of course I do! Come on! Let's eat lunch!

Yeah, well, I hadn't decided what I was going to do about that part yet. *Baby Steps*. That was the card to use. Maybe I couldn't do everything, but I could do something.

I started talking the minute we left Mr. V's room and Those Girls went into the restroom.

"I should have just given the kit back to Kylie without saying anything. I made things awful, and I hope you forgive me."

It came out like all one word and Tori blinked at me and Winnie gave a nervous giggle and Mitch scrunched up her face and Ophelia said, "*What* are you even talking about?"

I started to repeat it, but Tori shook her head at me. "Where did you get Kylie's kit thingy in the first place?"

"I found it," I said, which was the truth.

"Where?" Ophelia said, twisting the end of her braid.

"Outside," I said.

Mitch got all scowly. "That's weird."

"I know, huh?"

She didn't grunt. I was not okay right now.

"I didn't know the bra was in there and I didn't know the zipper thing was gonna come open and I didn't plan for it to go flying through the air and land . . . where it did."

Ophelia passed her hand over her mouth like she was erasing a smile.

"It's probably okay," Tori said. "We can talk to Lydia about it. You're still coming after school, right?"

"Coming where?"

Kylie. Right behind me.

"Are you having a party after school?" she said, all smiley and innocent. "Can I come?"

I wanted to climb into the garbage can. Tori looked right at her. "We're having a meeting about the Code. You can come if you want. Anybody can."

"Maybe I will." Kylie scattered her hair over the side of her face and tossed it back. All three of Those Girls did the same thing behind her. "Is it at your house, Tori?"

I could almost hear Ophelia's teeth crunching together. I absolutely heard Mitch grunt and Winnie whimper.

Only Tori's voice stayed calm. "Actually, yes. You know where I live."

"Okay then!"

Kylie motioned for her friends to follow her, and they continued on down the hall, but as she passed me, Kylie pinched the side of my hand. She might as well have just shouted, "You can't hang out with them *anywhere,* so don't even think about it."

"You don't think she'll come, do you?" Winnie whispered when they were gone.

"No," Ophelia said. "I mean, she won't, right?"

"Right," Tori said as they disappeared around the corner toward the cafeteria. "But I wonder what that was all about. I mean, (a) you know she still can't stand us and (b) she definitely doesn't care about the Code because she won't even sign it. So why even ask?"

"So she can come sabotage the meeting?" Ophelia said.

Mitch grunted louder. "She isn't *that* stupid."

"You know what?" I said.

They all looked at me as if they'd forgotten I was there.

"I don't feel good. I'm gonna go lie down in the nurse's office."

"Are you okay?" Winnie said.

No. I wasn't. I shook my head and went in the direction of the nurse's office. As soon as I knew the Tribelet was out of the hall, I doubled back and slipped into the restroom, where I closed myself into a stall and took out my sandwich. But after I looked at it for a minute, I put it back in the bag and waited for the bell to ring for fifth period. On the way there, I dumped it into the trash can.

Now I had to figure out how to avoid the Tribelet for the rest of the day. As I made my way to my seat, I realized that was going to be hard because, in one lunch period, I'd gone so far backward that I didn't even know which way I was facing. When I heard Mrs. Fickus call my name from the classroom doorway, I knew from the way her eyebrows were pointing up that she'd called me at least twice.

I got up to go to her, but she said, "Bring your books, Miss Hollingberry."

One of the BBAs whispered, "Busted," but she didn't hear it or that kid would have gone right past go and into lunch detention. Even before the Code, people behaved in Mrs. Fickus's class.

She waited for me in the hall. By that time, my palms were already so sweaty I could hardly hold on to the strap of my backpack. Even when she smiled at me, spreading out her always rosy-colored lips, I didn't feel any less dread. I mean, why would I?

"Ginger, honey," she said.

Wait. Did she just call me by my first name? And did she say *honey*? She *was* from the South, Louisiana or someplace, but she never used *honey* with us. And how come her head with its hair like yellow cotton candy was leaning in a sad way? Did something happen to Dad? Was she about to tell me something terrible? Did Those Girls tell her something?

I wanted to run. Instead I flattened myself against the wall.

"I owe you an apology," she said.

I shook my head for no reason.

"I do. I have completely underestimated you, and I haven't challenged you."

I didn't get it.

"Let me show you something." She opened the vanilla-colored folder she'd been pressing against her, which I probably hadn't noticed because it was the same color as her sweater. "These are your scores on the standardized tests you took at your last school, right before you came here."

"In Fresno," I said, because I felt like I should say something.

"Right. I just got these yesterday. Have you seen them?"

"No." I wasn't even sure what she was talking about.

She nodded for me to look at the numbers on the page, and I tried to act like I knew what they meant. Which I didn't. All I could think was, *Is she going to take me out of the smart classes?* We weren't supposed to know we were in them, but we all did.

"What this says, honey, is that you are reading on a twelfth-grade level." Mrs. Fickus looked at me like she was seeing me for the first time. "And your language skills aren't far behind that. Do you read a lot?"

Did I breathe?

"Yes," I said. "All the time."

I didn't add that the characters in my books were usually my only friends. She might think I was crazy instead of smart.

"All this time I've been teaching you like you're a sixth-grader, but I think it's time I changed that." She closed the folder and pressed it against her again. "Here's what I think we'll do. See if this sounds good to you."

"Okay," I said.

"Instead of doing this poetry unit with the rest of the class, how would you like to go to the library every day during this period and work on a special project with the librarian?"

"Just me?" I said.

"You and a student from one of my other sections. But you'll each be working independently."

I blinked several times until I was sure Mrs. Fickus thought I had stones in my eyes. Could I be hearing this right? On a day when everything else was all knotted up and bad, something good was happening to me?

"Is that a yes?" she said, drawing the *yes* out into about five syllables.

"Yes!" I said.

"All right then. Go on down to the library. You're expected." She squeezed the folder tighter. "And again, Ginger, I'm sorry I misjudged you. You're a bright girl. Don't hide that."

I might have to cross that off my list of Things Nobody Knows About Me.

As I made my way downstairs, I tried to remember the librarian. She was kind of a cranky lady, although maybe that was because she was going to have a baby. I read that in a book once. It didn't matter. As long as I was away from Those Girls and I didn't have to worry about the Tribelet *and* I could do a special project all by myself, the librarian could be the Witch-king of Angmar for all I cared.

When I got to the library, a man met me at the double glass doors. He had gray hair pulled back into a ponytail and wrinkled pants, and he was wearing clunky sandals. If he'd had a pointy hat and a long robe, he would've been identical to Gandalf. I liked him right away and wished he was one of my teachers. Like instead of Coach Zabriski.

When he nodded at me with a light in his eyes that were just a shade bluer than gray, I thought he might possibly be as cool as Mr. V. Only in a way more serious way. I found myself hoping that he wouldn't smile and spoil it.

"Are you Ginger?" he said.

I loved his voice too. It was kind of raspy, like he could probably do a really good imitation of Donald Duck.

"Yes," I said.

"I'm Mr. Devon."

"Are you a teacher?" I said.

The skin around his eyes crinkled into fans. "No. I'm the new librarian."

"A boy librarian?" I said.

"A girl scholar?" he said.

I expected to get that blotchy feeling, but I saw right away that he wasn't making fun of me.

"I just never met one before," I said.

"I *have* met girl scholars before," he said. "But never one as charming as you. Shall we?"

He wafted his hand—characters in fantasies were always wafting, so I knew what that was—and I followed where it led, past a set of shelves to a round table. A boy was already sitting there.

"Ginger, I give you Colin Quillin. Colin, my boy, this is Ginger."

The kid looked up at me and smiled with half his mouth. He had silky blond hair that fell over one eye so he had to jerk his head to get it out of the way to see me through his round glasses. His skin was as pale as Winnie's, and even sitting down, he was taller than most sixth-grade boys.

"A gentleman stands up when a lady enters the room," Mr. Devon said.

It seemed to take Colin a minute to realize Mr. Devon was talking to him. He pushed the chair back, only it didn't slide on the carpet and he almost fell backward, and when he did stand up, his feet got tangled up. I could see why. They were huge. Sort of like Big Bird's.

"A handshake would be appropriate," Mr. Devon said.

I stuck my hand out and Colin stuck out his and they missed each other and it took us two more tries to finally get them together. Why they didn't slide off one another, I had no idea. His were as sweaty and slippery as mine.

Somehow, we got into our chairs, and Mr. Devon sat across from us with his hands folded. He had long fingers with tiny tufts of dark hair on the lower part of them, and he wore a ring with a design I recognized.

"That's a Celtic knot," I said.

"Yes," he said. "Colin and I were just discussing that. He appreciates the Celts as well."

I looked at Colin and he looked at me and we both looked away.

"Let's begin, shall we?" Mr. Devon said. "Each of you will work with me doing a project about your favorite book of all time." He held up his index finger. "As long as that book has depth and is well written. We are talking about good literature here. I'll give you some time to think about it—"

"*The Lord of the Rings!*" I blurted out, my bullhorn fully operational.

But I wasn't the only one. Colin said the same thing. And just as loud.

"Really?" I said to Colin.

"Seriously?" he said to me.

"Brilliant!" Mr. Devon said to both of us.

It was actually. I had never met anybody my age who had even read it. Jackson thought it was lame, and I never brought it up with anyone outside the family. Even though I started my journey with it in fourth grade.

"Then may I make a suggestion?" Mr. Devon said.

"Yes, sir," Colin said.

Yes, sir. I liked that. I might start saying it.

"I'd like to propose that you do this project together rather than separately."

It didn't really sound like a question, so I nodded right away. Colin was slower, but he didn't look like he was going to throw up or anything when he said, "That makes sense."

"Good then," Mr. Devon said.

I looked at Colin. He looked at me. I watched his pale skin turn pink from his neck all the way up to his hair follicles. My own blotches were so hot, I almost searched for a fire extinguisher.

"It's settled." Mr. Devon gave a satisfied nod. "Now, will you each take out paper and pencil and write down why *The Lord of the Rings* is your favorite book?"

"How long can it be?" I said.

His lips twitched. "No more than the length of the trilogy itself."

Colin kind of laughed, and we sneaked another look at each other and both turned red again. I was going to have to bring a fan next time.

I wrote fast and filled up two and a half pages and only stopped then because my hand was hurting. Mr. Devon told me I could browse around the library while he read it.

"May I use a computer?" I said.

"Of course," he said.

I glanced at the clock. There was just enough time for me to get on my e-mail and write to Tori. Maybe it was because I'd forgotten about the whole situation for the last half hour that my mind wasn't jumbled like our kitchen junk drawer now. Kylie said I couldn't hang out with my Tribelet, but she didn't say I couldn't e-mail them, and I couldn't just let them think I didn't like them anymore. Not after all they did for me.

I remembered how to get on, and I started right in.

Dear Tori,

I hope you guys don't think I hate—

No, they wouldn't think that.

I deleted that part and started again.

I'm sure you're all wondering why I'm acting weird, like I don't want to be with you. I do. It's just that—

"You get to play on the computers?"

I jerked my face up to look at Kylie who was standing behind the screen, staring straight at me. My fingers fumbled over the keys, and I signed out.

"I'm sorry," she whispered. She waved a hall pass at me. "I came down here to check out a book and I saw you and I wanted to say . . ."

She glanced around and moved to squat beside me. I was so stiff and tight, I was afraid I'd crack.

"I wanted to say that if you keep doing what you're doing, we won't tell any more about your mother."

"You mean any more lies?" I whispered back before I could stop myself.

Kylie's eyebrows went up. Ophelia said she waxed them. I didn't care if she completely shaved them off right now.

"How do you know they're lies?" she said. "You told us yourself you didn't know how the accident happened or who she was with. But we can find out stuff like that."

"How?" I said.

Kylie looked at the computer screen. "You can find out anything on the Internet. Weren't you looking up something just now?"

"No," I said. "I was writing an e-mail."

As soon as it was out of my mouth, I wanted to flush myself down the nearest toilet. Why did I *tell* her that? Was I ever going to be able to stop everything I thought from blaring out of me?

"Sorry I interrupted you," Kylie said. "Sign back on."

"I'm done," I said.

"I feel bad now. Sign back on, seriously." She leaned against me like I was her new BFF. "I'm trying to be nice."

No wonder she could get people to do whatever she wanted them to do. All she wanted right now was to see who I was writing to. But I'd deleted it, and besides, I didn't feel like getting into a fight I wasn't going to win.

Still, my fingers shook as I typed in my password and got back to my e-mail account. I had no new messages and nothing in my out-box.

"I feel better now," Kylie said. "Go ahead and write. Or you could do it when you get home. Right after school."

She looked straight into my eyes and then she stood up and walked away. Message delivered.

We had a test in Spanish class, so I couldn't talk to anybody, which was a relief. As soon as the bell rang, I headed straight for my locker. I could be halfway home before either Those Girls or the Tribelet got out of the Spanish room.

But I wasn't fast enough. I just finished cramming all my books into my backpack and slamming my locker door when a shadow fell over me. I looked up at Mitch. She scowled down at me. Nobody could scowl like Mitch Iann.

"I gotta go," I said.

"Not 'til we talk," she said. Well, growled.

"No, really."

I darted around her. She followed me to the end of the locker hall and got past me, stopping me in the corner just before the steps. Unless I wanted to crawl between her legs, I was trapped.

"We had a meeting at lunch," she said.

"Sorry I couldn't be there."

"We said if you didn't want our help anymore, we would back off." Mitch crossed her arms so her hands went into the opposite armpits. "But we don't get why you won't tell us to our face."

Because I *can't*!

That's what I wanted to shout until it echoed through the stairwell. But all I could say was, "Sorry."

"Not good enough," Mitch said. "Not for me."

"Sor—"

"It would be one thing if you just wanted to stand up for yourself now, like Lydia said you'd have to eventually do, back when we first started this." Mitch gave one of her grunts. "But that's not what you're doin', is it?"

No! I was protecting my dad and my brother.

Wait. Mitch would get that, right? She punched somebody *out* for her brother. Maybe if I told her . . .

"What's this about?"

I wrenched my neck to look down the stairs where Mr. Jett was coming up. He had one of those shiny bald heads with black fringe around the edges that matched his toothbrush mustache. It was his eyes behind his glasses that made me think of a Doberman. That and his voice that was like a warning bark. All the time.

He reached us on the landing and pierced those eyes into Mitch. "You giving her a hard time? We have rules against that around here now."

"I was just talkin' to her," Mitch said, in a voice so low I almost had to read her lips to know what she was saying.

"Is that right?" Mr. Jett said to me.

"Yes, sir," I said.

"You don't have to run scared anymore."

"I'm not scared. Honest."

Mr. Jett nodded, but he didn't look like he was convinced.

"Why don't you move on along?" he said to Mitch. And then he stared at her until she grunted silently—I could see it in her neck—and went down the steps.

Mr. Jett waited until she disappeared below before he said, "Anything you want to tell me now?"

"No, sir," I said. "We really were just talking. About something serious."

"Is that why she looked like she was about to deck you?"

"She wasn't! Mitch wouldn't do that!"

"All right. Don't get all worked up."

Yeah, well, it was too late for that. My stomach was in a Celtic knot. Could this man go away so I could go after Mitch and tell her because she was the only person who would understand?

"Can I please go?" I said.

Mr. Jett looked like he was going to start a whole lecture, but just then a locker slammed above us and somebody shrieked. It was just a sixth-grader, but Mr. Jett took off two steps at a time, yelling, "What's going on up here?"

I took off down the steps and stitched my way through the crowd in the hall, jumping up every couple of steps to try to see Mitch. I finally spotted her spiky head at the front door, and I bullhorned, "Mitch! Wait up!"

"Are you *serious*?" someone said right behind me.

I shouldn't have turned around to answer Heidi. I should have kept going. I knew right then I should.

But Heidi wrapped her fingers around my wrist and held on, all the time smiling in that plastic way that reminded me of Mr. Potato Head so nobody would know she was about to say something mean. She put her goopy lips close to my ear.

"You were going to talk to *Michelle*?" She didn't wait for me to answer. "Kylie's going to hear about this."

She let go of me, and turned with a flip of her streaky hair that was too thin to swing like Kylie's did, and melted into the throng of kids headed the other way. Me, I just found the wall and pressed against it until the hall was empty. Then I walked home, without dreaming of being rich in the Gold Rush days. That kind of good thing never happened to me.

Chapter Five

On Saturday morning, I remembered that one good thing *had* happened to me that week, so I spent most of the weekend rereading my favorite parts of *The Lord of the Rings* to be ready for Colin and Mr. Devon on Monday.

As always, sitting on my Hobbit Seat, sinking into my favorite book made me want to be brave like Frodo, even though he was scared half to death. Even when he and Sam got separated from the Fellowship, they kept going, kept trying to get to Mordor where they could destroy the ring that made everybody evil. They didn't always have Gandalf to guide them, just the way I didn't have Lydia right now, so they had to trust other people to give them information.

Like the creature Gollum himself.

That, of course, made me think of Jackson, and then it dawned on me. Just because I couldn't talk about the accident to Dad didn't mean I couldn't talk to him. Dad always told him stuff he didn't tell me, even though he was only a year and a half older. Sure, Jackson would go into his cave again, but Grandma wouldn't take us away because of that.

I waited until after church Sunday when Dad went out to buy us a grill. Jackson was in his room, but his door was halfway open and he didn't have his ears blocked off with headphones or his face in a screen. He was sitting in the middle of his bed with a sketch pad, and since he didn't look like he wanted to pinch somebody's head off, I stepped inside.

"Yeah, don't bother to knock," he said, without looking up.

I glanced around for somewhere to sit down, but he had stuff on the chair, the bed, even the floor. It always looked like robbers had come in and ransacked the place. I took a chance and perched on the corner of the bed. He stared at it as if I had just dumped poison on his mattress.

"Is this okay?" I said.

"Whatever. Did you want something or did you just come in here to bug me?"

"I want to ask you a question."

"So ask it. Wait." He tapped the pad with his pencil. "You want to know if I'm drawing this for my girlfriend. The answer is yes. It's my marriage proposal."

He wasn't in a bad mood. Maybe we could have an actual conversation.

"You *could* have a girlfriend," I said. "You're not that ugly."

Jackson finally looked at me, his whole face twisted into a question mark. I sometimes thought the question mark was actually shaped the way it was because of the look Jackson gave me when he thought I was nuts.

"Whatever you want, the answer is no."

"Do you know what happened in mom's accident?"

Jackson got really still. The whole room did. The only thing that moved was his Adam's apple going up and down in his thin neck.

"She died," he said.

"I know, but why? Was it the person's fault that was driving?"

"I don't know."

"Who was it?"

"I said I don't *know*!"

I slid off the bed. Jackson tossed his sketch pad aside and leaned over to look at me on the floor.

"It doesn't matter," he said in a tight voice. "So stop asking questions."

"But I need to know."

"No, you don't. She's gone. We gotta move on." His face was white and his lips were almost blue. "Close the door on your way out."

I struggled to my feet, but I couldn't leave. It was like my feet were Velcroed to the rug. "If you ever find out, will you tell me?"

"Go."

"But I need—"

"There's two letters in that word. *G*. And *O*. Which one don't you understand?"

His voice was shaking hard, like he was going to cry in a minute and then I would start bawling and then—

"Hey."

I stopped in the doorway and looked back at him.

"Don't ask Dad. He's finally acting okay, and if you bring it up, he'll go back to like he was. You have to swear."

He really was going to cry. That was the only reason I said, "Okay. I swear."

That was it then. I couldn't get the truth to fight Those Girls with. I couldn't upset Dad or my brother. I couldn't go to Mitch or any of the rest of the Tribelet because every way I tried, Kylie knew about it. The only thing I could do was not make her mad.

So Monday morning, March 16, I told myself all the way to school that I would do whatever she wanted until . . . until when? How long was this going to go on?

A huge wave of something dark washed over me, just as I pushed through the front doors of the school. The first thing I saw was the Code, hanging on the wall. I had put so much hope into it. Now I wasn't sure it did any good at all.

The only thing I *could* hope for was my session with Lydia during lunch, although Kylie was going to be there too. Did she have to be *everywhere*? Maybe there would be other kids who'd violated the Code and it wouldn't be just us two. But then I'd never get to talk to Lydia.

It was like the only card in my pocket was *Save the Tears*. I did. When lunchtime came, I practically ran to the conference room in the library so I could at least see Lydia for a minute by myself. But I stopped in the doorway to regroup. It had only been a few weeks since I'd seen her, yet in that time I'd almost forgotten that she was a dwarf.

For real.

She'd told us she would rather be called a Little Person. Even smaller than Winnie, she was tiny everywhere except her head, which looked too big for her body, especially because of all the black curly hair. I had to look down at her as she came toward me, but I noticed right away that something was different.

"You don't walk funny anymore!" I said.

"Hello to you too," she said.

"Sorry," I said. "You just walk normal now. That's good, right?"

"That's very good. The surgery corrected my limp."

"I'm happy to see you," I said. And then the tears I'd been saving pushed their way out.

"And I'm happy to see you too. Very happy."

As I smeared at my eyes with the backs of my hands, I expected Lydia to ask me why I was avoiding the Tribelet. I knew they'd probably talked to her about it yesterday at the meeting at Tori's that I didn't show up for even though I said I would. But she didn't ask, because Kylie sauntered in (that's the only word for *that* walk), swishing her hair around. It said, *Even though I'm here because I have to be, I intend to take over.*

I looked away so she wouldn't see me smile. I hadn't had a reason to grin for, like, four days, but just thinking about how Lydia was going to make the smirk disappear from Kylie's face made me want to go, "Woo-hoo!"

"You must be Kylie," Lydia said.

She put out her hand for Kylie to shake it, but Kylie just stood there staring at her like she was an alien from Saturn.

"Let's get this out of the way," Lydia said. "I was born with dwarfism, which makes me one of the Little People. Other than that, I'm just like everyone else."

No, she's not, I wanted to say. She's not like anybody else you will ever meet, and you are about to find that out.

Kylie seemed kind of scared, as in she didn't shake Lydia's hand and she raised one shoulder like little kids do when they're afraid of a stranger.

"It's just going to be the three of us," Lydia said, "so I thought we'd sit over here."

She pointed to a trio of chairs she'd arranged by the window with a little low table in the middle, like we were going to have tea, only without the tea. As I followed Lydia over there, I wondered why there weren't more people here. Either everybody was following the Code or the teachers weren't enforcing it.

I sat down, but Kylie didn't. She pulled a pink gel pen out of the pocket of her jeans that were so skinny I didn't see how she could fit anything in there. "I won't be here that long," she said. "I just came down to sign the Code. That's the only reason I'm here."

Lydia patted the empty chair. "Go ahead and sit down for a minute. I don't happen to have a copy of the Code on me right now, so you might as well stay."

"It's posted in the front hall," Kylie said. Her hair said, *Are you clueless or what?*

"I know," Lydia said.

She looked at the chair and then at Kylie and then back at the chair. Kylie flounced herself into it.

Talk about clueless.

"You're actually not just here to sign the Code," Lydia said to her. "You were involved in a situation in P.E. that raised some concerns for the coach."

"It wasn't *my* situation," Kylie said.

"Tell me about it," Lydia said.

For the first time, I squirmed. What was Lydia doing?

Lydia gave me the tiniest of all nods, and I sat still. I would get my chance.

"I'll tell you exactly what happened," Kylie said.

Her voice had changed from Brussels sprouts bitter to sickeningly sweet. Like that fake sugar my dad put in his coffee.

"I was just sitting there talking to my friends first period about how I 'lost' my makeup kit."

"You say 'lost' like you don't believe that's what happened." Lydia smiled her smile that was like a slice of orange. "If you're going to tell exactly what happened, tell us everything."

"I don't want to accuse anybody of anything," Kylie said, eyes wide. "But I don't see how I could have lost it. I always keep it in my bag. A lot of people want my nice things and they're jealous of me." She looked down at her lap like she was trying to be shy. "That's all I want to say on that."

"All right. Go on."

"So, we were talking, and Ginger came over. My friend Heidi thought she wanted another makeover like we gave her the day before." Another Barbie doll smile. "You should have seen her. She looked so good. Anyway, Heidi told her we couldn't give her one because my makeup kit was missing. And then Ginger pulled it out from under her T-shirt . . ." Kylie demonstrated with an invisible case. "And she held it out like this, like she was taunting me." She put her hand to her chest, fingers spread out. "I was surprised because we were all so nice to her the day before. I didn't want to make a scene in front of the class, so I just said, you know, 'Give it to me,' and she wouldn't." Kylie lowered her gaze to her knees again. Her eyelashes almost brushed her face. "I didn't want to get Ginger in trouble because she's been trying so hard lately, but it *was* my makeup kit, so I did grab at it. I guess the zipper came open and . . ."

"And?" Lydia said. I couldn't tell from her face whether she was believing Kylie or not. "This is kind of embarrassing," Kylie said. "But I had a bra in there, and when the zipper came open, it popped out and I guess Ginger slung it down the bleachers so it would land in one of the boys' laps. Then they were all grabbing for it, and I just wanted to crawl in a hole, y'know?"

My mouth had never hung open that far. My chin was just about touching my collarbone. If I had been counting the lies, I would have run out of fingers.

"So, you can see why I shouldn't even be here," Kylie said.

"Because you're the victim," Lydia said.

"Well, not the victim." Kylie pulled *her* chin in as if Lydia had just suggested she had pimples.

"We'll get to that in a minute." Lydia turned to me. If she noticed I was one big blotch, she didn't say. "Your turn, Ginger. Tell us what happened."

"I just *told* you!" Kylie said.

"You told us how you saw it. I want to hear both sides." Lydia smiled. "There are always two. Ginger?"

I didn't even get my lips moving before there was a tap on the door. A lady I recognized as the school secretary poked her head in when Lydia said, "Yes?"

"I need to see you," she said.

Lydia paused for a second, and then she sighed and climbed down from her chair. "Will you ladies sit quietly for a minute?"

"Absolutely," Kylie said.

And then of course the second the door clicked shut, she turned on me, eyes down to hard lines.

"I heard you were talking to Michelle Iann." Kylie pushed her neck toward me. "Haven't you had enough warning? Are you, like, dense?"

The door opened, and Kylie pulled her neck back like a turtle and plastered on the Barbie smile again.

"Kylie," Lydia said, "your mother is here to take you to your dentist appointment."

The hair flipped in triumph, and Kylie slipped from the chair. "I'll sign the Code on the way out," she said, and left.

I slumped. Lydia stood in front of me, hands folded.

"All right, Ginger," she said. "It's just you and me. Do you want to tell me what's really going on?"

Did I want to? Did I breathe the air?

Actually, I didn't breathe at that moment. I felt like I was being ripped in half right down the middle. I could trust Lydia, but then what? If she did anything about it, Kylie would know I told.

"You're obviously miserable, my friend," Lydia said.

I blinked hard. "I can't tell you everything."

"Then tell me what truth you can. It won't leave this room."

"Really?"

"Really—unless someone is physically hurting you."

I wondered if the knotted-up pain in my stomach counted.

"I can't tell you why," I said, "but I'm still afraid of Kylie. I try to stand up to her, but it's not working and I feel stupid about it. You and Tori and everybody helped me, and now I can't even . . ." Can't even finish the sentence.

"We can't expect things to change like that. " Lydia snapped her tiny fingers. "And here's the thing: it's natural for you to still feel uncertain after all you've been through. Telling you not to have a reaction to the meanness of those girls is like telling one of those leaves out there not to blow in the wind. You can't expect yourself not to feel anything."

"So, my stomach hurting is normal?"

"It's a normal reaction to an abnormal situation." Lydia shook her wonderful curls. "It's important for you to remember that the problem isn't with you, Ginger, it's with Kylie." Her eyebrows twitched. "She's quite the actress, but that doesn't make her better than you. Nothing makes her better than you. Until you realize that, the bullying—whatever it is right now—will continue and you'll remain powerless."

I'd always loved the way Lydia talked to us like we were adults.

"I'm going to respect your right not to tell me anything, although I hope at some point you will. But I think I can help you."

"Please?" I said.

"Let me ask you this first: have you talked to your dad about what's going on?"

"No!"

She pushed her hands down to show me I needed to get calm. I tried, but not telling my dad was the whole *point*.

"I don't mean all the details," Lydia said. "But if we're going to fight bullying, it can't all be up to you. Teachers have to help, and so do parents." She nodded at me like she wanted me to nod too. "Maybe I'll ask him to join us one day for lunch. Did you bring yours today, by the way?"

"I'm not hungry," I said. I might never be again.

She looked at me for a few seconds, like she was deciding what to say, and then she picked up her cell phone from the table. I thought she was going to call Dad right then, but she said to me, "Meanwhile, let's you and I get to work. Here's a good Baby Step for you."

"Okay," I said.

"I'm going to teach you how to make a neutral face. We'll call it a 'Stone Face.'" She held up the phone. "Make the face you make when Kylie is being mean to you."

That was easy. Even thinking about it made my eyes all darty and my head twitchy and my mouth weird like I was about to barf. I didn't realize Lydia was going to take a picture until it was too late.

"Now," she said, "see if you can erase all expression and just look like a stone."

That was harder. It took me several tries before she snapped the pic.

"Check these out."

She held out the phone, and I looked at the shot of me in I'm-about-to-be-sick mode. It was pretty pathetic.

"Now this one."

I almost didn't recognize myself without fear smeared all over me.

Lydia tilted her head at me. "So tell me, Ginger: which one of these girls is less likely to be picked on?"

"Stone Face," I said.

"There you go," she said.

Lunch was over by then, and I felt, well, a Baby Step better. I wasn't sure looking at Kylie like she wasn't there would help a whole lot, but I didn't have time to think about it because Colin came into the library and Mr. Devon joined us at our table and it was suddenly like we were at the Council of Elrond.

"I was quite impressed with both your papers," Mr. Devon said. "I've used what you wrote to come up with a five-step plan for you to use to discover your project."

"We're going to discover it?" Colin's voice sounded like we were about to fly off to Mordor. He was so not like the other boy creatures I knew. There wasn't even a hint of a burp or a belch. I wasn't sure Colin even *had* armpits.

"You are," Mr. Devon said. "Does that please you?"

We both nodded. What pleased me was the way he talked to us. It was like we were *in* Middle Earth.

Mr. Devon turned over a big piece of paper that was on the table and resituated it so Colin and I could both see it while he looked at it upside down. Five steps were listed there:

Step One: Share with each other what makes *The Lord of the Rings* your favorite book.

Step Two: Determine how Tolkien makes it so brilliant.

Step Three: Discover what the STORY is about (not the plot) and state it in one sentence.

Step Four: Apply that to your own life in some way.

Step Five: Create a storyboard for a tale that expresses that life lesson, using what you've learned from Step Two about developing a brilliant story.

"Do you have any questions?" Mr. Devon said.

"How did *you* get to be so brilliant?" I said. "This is the most awesome project I've ever heard of."

"How much time do we get?" Colin said. He was wiggling his legs, like he thought it was as awesome as I did.

"Oh, yeah. That would be good to know."

Mr. Devon rubbed his hands together like he was about to eat a steak. "April 14 is the Fifth-Grade Fair. All the fifth-graders in Grass Valley who are going to be sixth-graders here next year are coming to find out what's in store for them."

"Poor kids," Colin said.

Mr. Devon didn't seem to hear that. "If what you come up with is brilliant enough, you will be allowed to present it at the fair."

"You mean, like, read them our story?" I said.

"That's a possibility," Mr. Devon said.

He looked at Colin.

"Oh," I said. "Sorry—I should've asked you. I don't know—do you like to read out loud—I mean, I do but—"

"I sort of do," Colin said.

Then of course we turned the color of a pair of tomatoes—me in splotches, him in one big flood.

Mr. Devon tapped the paper. "I'll leave you two to get started on Step One. You can decide the rest later."

"Yes, sir," Colin said.

I wanted to thank him for giving me the idea to say "sir" because it had helped me with Mr. Jett the day before, but I decided not to. He probably thought I was weird enough already.

"I'll get my binder," I said instead.

I really couldn't wait to get started, and I almost got tangled up in the table leg getting to my backpack. When I returned to the table, Kylie was standing on the other side of it.

Okay, so *that* was the shortest dentist appointment ever.

She didn't say anything. She didn't have to. Her bob said it for her: *Do you see that not even your Lydia person is going to stop me?*

But Lydia's words were louder than Kylie's hair. *Which one of these girls is less likely to be picked on?*

It took everything I had, but I formed the Stone Face.

Kylie's eyes bugged and her lip curled and her hair smacked into the side of her face as she huffed away. As soon as she was gone, I deflated.

"I feel your pain."

I looked up as Colin slid into the chair beside me.

"What?" I said.

"I said I feel your pain." He shrugged. "We should get to work."

"Yeah," I said. I straightened in the chair. "We should."

Chapter Six

The next few days were the worst for me since I started at Gold Country Middle School. Worst as in I walked around with a big hurting knot in my stomach.

It wasn't because Kylie and Those Girls were being openly mean to me like they used to be. They weren't. Even though I was the slowest person on our team in P.E. and I could only get up to the second knot on the ropes and I knocked every hurdle down trying to jump over it, nobody called me a name or rolled their eyes back into their sockets or said they wished I was back on the other team. At least they learned *something* from five days' suspension: don't let the teachers catch you.

Those days were the worst because I had to ignore Mitch when she tried to help me. And because Tori's team was all cheering for each other and telling Winnie, who was the second slowest in the class behind me, that she could do it.

It was because in our classes I watched them explain pre-algebra to each other and be each other's lab partners and do Spanish dialogues together to practice.

It was because even though Shelby and Evelyn invited me to eat lunch with them, I couldn't be in the cafeteria and watch what used to be *my* Tribelet share cookies and giggles and secrets I wasn't in on anymore. So, I skipped lunch and did homework in the library—the only place I felt safe. I couldn't eat anyway.

By Thursday morning, it was hard to even focus on the questions at the end of the social studies chapter. They were so easy that border collie on my street could've answered them, but all I could think about was that maybe it was always going to be this way whether I wore a Stone Face with Kylie or not. Whether I Saved the Tears or took Baby Steps or didn't do any of it, it might not matter.

In third period on Thursday, I got a pass to the restroom. I sat in the stall and decided maybe it would have been better if I'd never experienced friendship. It was almost worse than the bullying, because now I knew what I was missing.

I missed it so much, I could hardly stand how much it hurt.

Two things kept me from going all the way back to the way I was my first days there. One was my fifth-period meetings with Mr. Devon and Colin and J. R. R. Tolkien, when I could forget my bullies weren't as easy to defeat as Orcs. The other was looking forward to my Thursday meeting with Lydia. She might not be able to help me change things, but at least she liked me.

When I got to the library conference room at lunchtime, Lydia had the little table set with two plates and cups and napkins and, in the middle, her weird but wonderful hummus and grapes and snap peas and pita bread and olives and whole almonds.

"A little Greek feast for us," she said, smiling her orange-slice smile. "I'm hungry, and I didn't feel like eating alone."

I almost couldn't save the tears.

We talked about all kinds of other stuff while we ate, like my project in fifth period and what we liked about *The Lord of the Rings* movies and why things tasted better when you ate them with your fingers instead of a fork. I forgot I had a stomachache.

We were done in about ten minutes, and Lydia pulled a pad of yellow sticky notes and a green marker out of her red canvas bag that was almost bigger than she was.

"Do you mind if I put some of these on your clothes?" she said.

I giggled. "No! But why would you do that?"

"Bear with me. Will you stand up?"

I did.

"Now, tell me the names people call you. Think of them as the labels they put on you."

I didn't remind her we only had fifteen minutes left.

"Annoying," I said right away.

She wrote *Annoying* on one of the notes and stuck it on the front of my T-shirt.

"What else?"

"Loser," I said.

That went on a note and then on my shirt.

We continued with *Smelly, Not Girly, Loud, Obnoxious, Klutz, Weirdo, Fat, Freak, Bullhorn, Stupid,* and *Ugly.*

When I started repeating myself, Lydia stopped and had me look at my reflection in the window. The entire front of my shirt, plus my sleeves, was covered in yellow squares with green writing on them.

I felt my face crumple.

"Before you go there," Lydia said, "I want you to notice something: none of these labels is part of you. Not like your cute freckles or your pretty blue eyes or your great smile."

Cute? Pretty? Great? Was she serious?

"These are all labels *other* people have stuck on you. Do you see that?"

I sort of did. My nod was slow.

"Why the hesitation?" Lydia said.

"I don't know." I shrugged. "Maybe some of them are true."

"All right. Let's take them one by one. If you believe the label, I'll leave it there. If you don't—you truly don't—you *rip* it off."

I started with *Stupid.* "I'm really not," I said. "Maybe I look it, but—"

"That one's out of here," Lydia said. "Rip it off."

I did. She crumpled it into a ball and tossed it in the trash can.

"*Smelly* can go," I said. "I take a shower and wash my hair every day now. I didn't use to, but it's like people's noses have a memory or something."

"So . . ."

I ripped it off. I also decided *Weirdo* and *Freak* could go because Mr. Devon didn't seem to think I was either of those things for liking the things I liked.

I hadn't been *Loud* or *Obnoxious* for two days because, well, basically I hadn't said much at all. So I peeled those off, although I couldn't quite manage ripping.

"Let's see what we have left," Lydia said. "*Fat?*" She tugged at my T-shirt. "Looks like there's plenty of room in there to me."

"I don't think I'm fat," I said. "But they do."

"Who?"

"Those Girls."

"Are you willing to let them tell you what you are if you don't believe it yourself?"

"You could take it off, I guess."

Lydia shook her curls. "You're the one who has to decide it doesn't fit. Nobody else can do that for you."

I left it there. Same with *Not Girly,* although I didn't mind that one so much. And *Klutz,* because, let's face it. Maybe the same with *Bullhorn.* Maybe not.

And then there was *Ugly*.

"Take another look at that girl in the window," Lydia said. Her voice was all soft and kind, like she was talking to a kitten.

Just as I turned to face my reflection again, somebody knocked on the door. Loud.

While Lydia was crossing to answer it, I felt like I was naked. I tried to cover my five labels with my hands and got all twisted like a pretzel.

"Are you Lydia?" a voice said from the doorway.

"I am. And you are?"

"Pete Hollingberry. Ginger's father."

"Of course! Come in. We were just finishing up."

I turned away from the window just in time to see my dad looking down—way down—at Lydia. I guess I'd never mentioned to him that she was a dwarf.

But he didn't seem weirded out at all. Not like he did when he looked at *me* right then. The words *What the Sam Hill?* were written across his wrinkled-up forehead.

"We were just doing a little exercise," Lydia said. "Do you want to have a seat?"

Dad sat down, probably because standing up staring down at a Little Person was kind of hard on a tall person's neck.

"We're working on being who we are, rather than who people tell us we are." Lydia grinned. "I'm sure you're wondering about the sticky notes. Ginger, do you want to tell your dad?"

"This is about bullying?" Dad said.

I felt Blotch Number One form on my neck.

"It's about *anti*-bullying," Lydia said. She didn't act like somebody had just been rude to her, which, in my opinion, he had.

"You going to teach her how to fight back?" Dad said. "She's never been able to do that. Lets people walk all over her."

Blotch Number Two. Left cheekbone.

Lydia cocked her big head of hair. "We think of it as taking back the power to be ourselves so other people don't have power over us."

Dad nodded, but not like he was agreeing with her. "Ignore it and let it pass. I can support that."

Blotches Three and Four. Both at once on my forehead and chin.

"Kids grow out of it," Dad said. "I got called Carrot Head 'til I was fifteen. I survived."

All the blotches grew together. My whole head was steaming.

"Are you a Jesus kind of guy, Mr. Hollingberry?" Lydia said.

What? What kind of question was that?

But Dad sat up straighter, and his eyes lit up like little birthday candle flames.

"I am," he said.

"I thought so." Lydia folded her hands and looked all relaxed in her chair. "I don't recall Jesus ever saying, 'Fight back,' or 'Ignore bullying and it'll go away.'"

Did Jesus talk about bullying at all? What Bible was she reading? I never heard that in church.

"Ginger," Lydia said, "would you mind waiting outside for a few minutes while I chat with your dad?" She looked at him. "That all right with you?"

"Good idea," he said.

I thought it was the worst idea ever. But at least this way my head wouldn't burn right off my shoulders.

Still, when the door shut behind me, I sat in the chair right next to it. Okay, I wasn't supposed to hear what they were saying or Lydia wouldn't have asked me to leave. But y'know, I was feeling shut out, left out, and pushed out, and my stomach was starting to hurt again. So I listened. I could only hear snippets.

LYDIA: Have you ever had a difficult boss?

DAD: (with a laugh that sounded like a hard "huh") Got one right now . . . everything that's conflict isn't bullying.

LYDIA: . . . Right. Bullying is consistent degradation of a person. On purpose . . . put-downs . . . over and over . . . had my share when I was younger.

DAD: Can see how you would've.

LYDIA: Ginger shouldn't have to. Nobody should.

DAD: . . . build character?

LYDIA: Or resentment. Anger. Fear. Self-hatred.

DAD: (silence)

LYDIA: . . . all in this together . . . teachers and parents and kids . . . won't just go away by itself.

"Ginger!" someone whispered.

I almost put my hands up to surrender. Busted. Why was I the one who always got caught?

But the person who whispered my name again poked her head out of an aisle of books and I saw that it was Shelby. Tall Shelby who moved like the branches of a willow tree.

"Come here," she said. Her plumpy lips hardly moved, so I wasn't sure I really heard it.

She crooked her finger at me, and I hurried over, looking behind me the whole time. Just habit.

"Can you meet me in here after school?" she said.

She wasn't one of Those Girls anymore. Her pale blue eyes hadn't squinted in weeks, as far as I knew, and she invited me to sit with her and Evelyn at lunch without acting like it was some duty she had to perform. But that could all change in one hour with Kylie around.

"Why?" I said.

"I just need to talk to you." Shelby lowered her voice even more and brought her head down too so she had to talk through a veil of reddish-blond hair. "Kylie and Riannon and all of them are trying out for seventh-grade cheerleading after school. They won't be around, so you don't have to worry."

"I have to ask my dad," I said.

"Ask me what?"

I must have bullhorned even when I was trying to whisper.

Dad stood at the end of the book aisle, freckly arms folded and mouth in a straight line. I knew he wasn't mad. That was just how he looked. Shelby might not know that, though.

"Um—this is Shelby," I said, sort of waving my arm in her direction. "She wants to know if we can talk after school, so I might get home later than you say to."

I stopped because I wasn't sure I was making any sense. Where was that sticky note that said *Weirdo*?

I looked down at my shirt. *Klutz, Not Girly, Fat, Ugly,* and *Bullhorn* were still in place. Aw, *man.* I folded *my* freckly arms over them, but Shelby's eyes were on Dad.

"Can she, please?" she said. "I really need to talk to her."

Dad almost smiled, and if I hadn't known better, I would've thought his eyes were wet. But I knew better.

"'Course she can," he said, and looked at me like I was a new puppy. "You and your friend talk. Just be home by four."

He left and Shelby left, and through the open door, I saw Lydia packing up the food. I pulled the labels off my shirt and pushed them into my pocket.

We had an assembly fifth period so Colin and I didn't get to work together, which I would rather have been doing than listening to somebody talk about drinking and drugs, which we'd all been hearing about since we were in second grade. I'd gotten it twice a year because of all the moving around.

In Spanish, Mrs. Bernstein was absent so we had study hall. I tried to do my social studies multiple choice assignment, but the As and Bs and Cs and Ds kept getting mixed up with what Shelby could possibly want to talk about. I gave up on that and made a new list to put in my private binder: *Things Other People Think About Me.* All the things Lydia had written on the labels went on the list. I even thought of some more: *Gullible. Rug.*

The bell finally rang, and I went straight to the library. Mr. Devon waved to me from behind the counter and said, "I missed our time together. Was the assembly enlightening?"

"Don't drink until you're twenty-one," I said, "and then don't get drunk or drive a car if you do."

"Duly noted," Mr. Devon said.

"Hi."

Before I could turn around, Shelby had her warm hand in mine. She pulled me past the rows of bookshelves to a table back in a corner. In spite of her telling me Kylie and her friends were off at tryouts, she looked over her shoulder through her hair about twelve times. It was like being in a spy movie. Did I look like that, all paranoid and nervous?

When Shelby finally sat down, she pulled her cell phone out of her backpack, and it was my turn to look around for spies.

"Mr. Devon doesn't let people have those in the library." I hoped my voice was a whisper. It had gotten me busted so many times, I didn't trust it anymore.

"I have to show you something." Shelby bunched her pretty lips as she tapped at the little screen with her thumbs and turned it to me. Only my dad had a cell phone at our house, and I never used it, so I wasn't sure what I was looking at.

Shelby pushed it closer. "See that message?"

"Uh-huh."

"That's what's going around on Twitter."

"What's Twitter?" I started to blotch. Add *Totally Out of It* to that list. "I've heard of it, but—"

"It's a website where somebody posts something and all the people who follow that person on Twitter get it. You need to read it."

Drunk driver killed Gingerbread's mom, it said. *Who was it? Post if you know. #TakeDownT.*

My stomach tried to come up my throat. "That's not true," I said.

"I totally believe you." Shelby looked at me through her panels of hair. "But her followers believe *her*."

"Whose followers?" I knew, of course, but . . . I pointed to *#Take-DownT.* My finger was shaking.

"That's so people will know what this is about."

"Shouldn't it say *Take Down G*?"

"I don't know." Shelby swished her finger across the screen and dropped the phone back into her pack. Her pale eyes looked long and sad. "The thing is, there are, like, eighty-three followers on this."

"There aren't even that many people in the whole sixth grade!"

"Shhh!"

I slapped my hand over my mouth, partly so I could hush myself and partly so I wouldn't throw up.

"There's a hundred and twenty," Shelby said. "The eighty-three is probably everybody who has a Twitter account."

She put her hand on top of mine on the table. I didn't know what to do about that, so I just stayed still. I could feel my palm sweat oozing into the wood.

"I'm not going to follow her now," she said. "I just kept it on there so I could show you and now I'm getting off. I'm not part of their group anymore, and I never want to be again."

She was starting to get teary-eyed. I pulled my hand away and fished in my jeans pocket, around the sticky notes, and brought out a Kleenex. It was all torn into tissue-lace, but it was clean, so I offered it to her. Shelby balled it up in her hand and let the tears slide down her cheeks.

"At least they leave me alone," she said. "But that's only because they can't get in any more trouble or they'll be expelled next time."

"What's the difference between getting suspended and being expelled?"

"If you're expelled, you don't get to come back for the rest of the year. Or maybe ever."

"For real?"

Shelby put her finger to her lips.

"For real?" I whispered.

She nodded. "After all that stuff happened and they got suspended, my parents came in and talked to Mrs. Yeats and told her they're monitoring the Kylie situation."

"How?"

"If Kylie or any of them is mean to me, all I have to do is tell my parents and they go straight to Mrs. Yeats."

"They totally have your back," I said. I wondered what that felt like.

"Yeah." Shelby bunched her lips again. "But they don't know how sneaky Kylie can be. I do. There's no way to trace that Twitter thing back to her because it's just a made-up Twitter name. She might even have her account linked to a fake e-mail address. I just wanted you to know what she can do without anybody ever catching her."

If this was supposed to be making me feel better, it was doing the exact opposite. My stomach found a new knot to tie itself into. Did my dad follow Twitter? Could he see this . . . *lie* eighty-three other people were seeing?

Shelby stared at her backpack for a minute—a really long minute—and I wasn't sure what I was supposed to do or say. When she finally looked back at me, her chin was straight and her eyes weren't teary anymore.

"You know what?" she said. "You and Tori Taylor and all of them, you're the ones who showed me how to get away from Kylie. Your Code thing was the only reason I told my parents everything. So I think you should do the same thing." She grabbed my sweaty hands. "Your dad seems really nice. You should tell him about this and have him go to Mrs. Yeats."

"I ca—"

"And you should sit with me and Evelyn at lunch. I don't *know* why you aren't hanging out with your friends anymore, but I *bet* it's because of Kylie, and I just totally think you should at least sit with *us*. Kylie won't bother you at our table or I'll tell my mom." She shrugged. "Simple, right?"

I wished it was. But as I sat there with my sweaty palms on the table, looking at Shelby doing the *Gold Thumb*, all I could think were the words she just said herself: *I just want you to know what Kylie can do without anybody ever catching her.*

If I hung out with Shelby and Evelyn, it would only be a matter of time—like one class period—before they'd be hurt. Everybody I even came close to ended up that way, including my own dad and brother. I couldn't do it to this girl who was being so nice to me.

"Thanks," I said. "I'll see."

Shelby's face drooped. So did my entire heart. We probably both knew I wouldn't do it.

She picked up her backpack and sort of smiled at me, and took her willowy self out of the library. I stared at my sweaty palm prints on the table until they disappeared.

"Can I be of assistance with something, Ginger?"

I looked up at Mr. Devon with his gray ponytail and his proper way of talking. He was probably a *Weirdo* in Kylie's eyes, so how did he do it? How did he just walk around being all real when people were rolling their eyes and thinking, *That guy's a freak?*

"Really, can I help?" he said.

"No, sir," I said, because there was only one person who could.

"Is it okay if I get on my e-mail?" I said.

"I'll stay open for a few more minutes, yes."

I thanked him and went to a computer and typed:

Dear Lydia,

Remember I told you about the five-step plan Mr. Devon gave us for our project? Do you think we could have one for me, for how I can be me without anybody bothering me? If you can't, I'll understand. But I think it would really help.

> *Sincerely,*
> *Ginger Hollingberry*

Maybe it was stupid and weird, but I clicked *send* anyway.

Chapter Seven

Shelby was right about one thing: everybody that used Twitter in our class had obviously gotten the Twitter message. The minute I walked into the gym locker room Friday morning I could feel the look-at-Ginger-look-away-quick thing going on. I wanted to crawl into my locker.

I got changed fast and went out to the gym so I could sit by myself and not see what people were thinking. As long as I couldn't look in their eyes, I wouldn't start believing it was true, about my mom being with a drunk driver. I didn't know what *was* true, but it just couldn't be that.

It was raining, so Coach and Mrs. Zabriski were setting up some of the obstacle course in the gym. I could hear them talking to each other since nobody else was in there. I, of course, was invisible.

"Who calls a faculty meeting on a Friday after school?" Coach barked at his wife.

"It's about this bullying thing everybody's making a big deal out of," she said.

Coach growled. Really, he did. "It's the girls. Boys just pound each other and it's over."

"I'd like to pound a few people myself," Mrs. Z said.

He growled again and motioned toward the bleachers with his head. Mrs. Zabriski looked at me as if I'd just crawled in from underneath them.

I put on my Stone Face.

I wore it all morning, and it worked. Nobody needled me about my mom or gave me lip-curled looks. Of course, nobody talked to me or basically even looked at me at all, and my stomach was in so many knots I lost count. But at least nobody bothered me.

At lunchtime, I even went into the cafeteria and sat at a table no one used and unwrapped my sandwich. We were out of peanut butter at home, so it was just pickle, which always helped when my stomach hurt. Sitting by myself brought on the blotches, but I was only on Number Two when I felt somebody standing over me.

"Can I sit with you?" said a voice that broke at the end.

I looked up and stared at Colin until I realized my mouth was open.

"Yeah," I said. "Of course. I'll move my stuff."

I rearranged my lunch and pushed out a chair for him with my foot and almost knocked it over, and it would have crashed to the floor if he hadn't caught it. It was totally surprising that he didn't change his mind and bolt.

Once he sat down, I stopped freaking out because it was just like it was in the library. Calm and not nervous and okay.

"Where do you usually sit?" I said.

"I don't," he said. "I find someplace to do homework or whatever. I hate coming in here."

He opened a plastic container that was shaped like a brown lunch bag and pulled out a sandwich in a Baggie. Mine was in Saran Wrap because Dad said Baggies were too expensive. Colin must be richer than us (who wasn't?), but he didn't look at my soggy sandwich and my bruised banana and curl his lip into a roll.

"I hate it in here too," I said. "Did you ever eat your lunch in the boys' bathroom?"

Colin shook his head. "I tried, but Mr. Jett made me come out."

"Oh," I said. "Did you ever pound anybody?"

"You mean like beat them up?"

"I guess so."

He shook his head again. I liked the way his hair fell over his eye and he had to nod it back. It reminded me of the silky stuff on an ear of corn.

"It's not worth it," he said.

He took a bite of his sandwich, which smelled like the peanut butter that was missing from mine.

"Did you ever try pickles with that?" I said.

Colin's mouth went up on one side. "Peanut butter and pickle?"

"It's my favorite," I said. "I only have pickle today."

"Can I try it?"

"You want some pickle for yours, you mean?"

"Yeah. Do you mind?"

"No. Here."

I pushed a slice of kosher spear across the table on the Saran Wrap and watched him slide it into the part of the sandwich with the bite out of it.

He smiled that half of a smile again. "I'm goin' in," he said and chomped into it.

"Well?" I said.

"Man, that is *good*." He put the other half of his sandwich on the wrap and pushed it back at me. "Have this. Put your other pickle on it."

"You sure?"

He chewed and nodded.

"Isn't this *cute*?"

Riannon's pointed voice.

"It *is*," I heard Heidi say—well, snort. "I didn't know you two were going out."

I let the pickle drop. But Colin looked straight at me, and he said, "So, I thought if we want to make our presentation thing epic, we should use all the time we have to work on it. I mean, right?"

I stared for a second, and then I said, "Right."

"Hel-lo-o, ru-ude," Riannon said.

Colin held my eyes with his like they were hands.

"Fine," Heidi said.

I imagined them flouncing off all huffy, but I didn't look. And I didn't look when one of the BBAs came by and made a kissing sound. Or when an entire table somewhere in the lunchroom all went, "Oooooh-ooh," at the same time. I just looked at Colin, who said, "So, you think? We work at lunch and fifth period and then whenever else?"

"I'm in," I said.

And I was pretty sure it didn't come out like I was using a bullhorn.

∾

We weren't the only ones getting ready for the Fifth-Grade Fair. Mrs. Bernstein told the whole class about it sixth period.

"We're responsible for the Spanish booth," she said. "We'll have Hispanic food and make some posters, maybe use costumes. Anything to show the fifth-graders that Spanish class isn't a torture chamber."

Mrs. Bernstein was sarcastic a lot, and she used her up-and-down velvety eyebrows and her sharp face to make it work. Sometimes it was pretty funny to me. When she wasn't pointing it *at* me.

"This is totally not a torture chamber," Kylie said without raising her hand. "You're our favorite teacher."

Mrs. Bernstein wasn't *my* favorite teacher, and I knew she wasn't the Tribelet's either. That was so Kylie. I kind of wanted to spit.

"I'm going to assign the jobs," Mrs. Bernstein said.

Tori raised her hand, and Mrs. Bernstein nodded at her, black ponytail swaying.

"We'll do whatever you want before the fair," Tori said. "But Winnie and Ophelia and Mitch and I have to be at the Anti-Bullying booth."

That dark wave washed over me again.

"Okay, let me make a note," Mrs. Bernstein said.

She picked up her clipboard, and Tori raised her hand again.

"Go on."

"And Winnie and I are doing a thing for Mr. Jett's science team too."

"That sounds thrilling," Riannon said. Right after Kylie poked her.

Tori smiled. "It is. I'm geeked out and proud *of* it."

Those Girls blinked at her like they were all wearing Riannon's contacts.

"Mrs. Bernstein." Mitch had her hand up this time.

"Señorita Michelle?"

"I gotta be in Coach's physical fitness demonstration." She waved her arm over the soccer girls. "All of us. And the BB—the boys."

The BBAs pumped the air and then punched each other like they just won the Super Bowl. The other guys in the class just sort of shrugged.

"Okay, checking all of you off."

Ophelia's hand waved.

"Señorita Smith?" Mrs. Bernstein said it like she was trying not to get irritated.

"Evelyn and Shelby and I are doing a social studies thing for Mr. Jett because . . . what he was going to put up there was kind of boring."

Mrs. Bernstein looked up from her clipboard. Her eyebrows went into upside down Vs. "I'm going to go with Tori's suggestion then. Each of you will have an assigned thing to bring or make for the booth, and that leaves, let's see, who to man it?" She ran her pencil down the paper. "Señoritas Kylie, Heidi, Riannon, and Izzy."

None of them even moved an eyelash back at her. Kylie made a hissing-in sound. Well, yeah, there *was* kind of a *you are the leftovers* feel to it. I had some of that going on myself. As in, Mrs. Bernstein hadn't mentioned my name at all.

Izzy, however, was on it, after the passed-on poking from Kylie down.

"What about Señorita Gingerbr—Ginger?" Izzy said, cheeks like wax apples.

Mrs. Bernstein looked straight at me. "Aren't you doing something special with Mr. Devon in the library?"

"*Sí,*" I said.

"Thank you for using your Spanish. All right, Señor Patrick and Señor Douglas, I want you to pass out the Hispanic Culture books— over there, on the top shelf . . ."

The class buzzed like they did when books were being handed out, and Mrs. Bernstein was doing something else, this time going to the door. Izzy's head popped up from the noise, and she said to me, "What are you doing with Mr. Devon?"

"Señorita Ginger." Mrs. Bernstein came down the aisle with a big brown envelope. "This just came for you."

For Ginger Hollingberry, the label said. *From Lydia Kiriakos.*

I wanted to open it so badly my fingers twitched, but I wasn't going to spoil whatever it was by letting Kylie or anybody else see it. If she tried to grab it from me . . . well, *I* could have gotten expelled.

Handling it very gently, I slid it into my backpack and made sure the zipper was all the way zipped. Safe.

Or not. Kylie was now in the desk next to mine, giving me the Barbie smile. My stomach squeezed.

"You must be so special now," she said, in a voice that made my bullhorn sound like a whisper. "You get to go to the library every day fifth period. You're doing something with Mr. Devon for the fair. And now you get a delivery right to class." Her eyes were so wide and innocent she looked like a Disney princess. "I want to know all about what you're doing."

I put on my Stone Face.

"You gotta be kidding me." Ophelia was in the middle of the aisle with her hands on her hips. Her bigger-than-anybody's eyes were on Kylie. "Kylie, that was the worst acting job I have ever seen. You didn't mean one single word of that."

Kylie's eyes went down into those slit things, until Mrs. Bernstein came down the other aisle saying, "Señorita *Smith*! That was uncalled for." Kylie immediately looked like someone had just taken away her birthday.

Ophelia was wrong. Kylie was a *great* actor. As always, she had Mrs. Bernstein fooled.

"Lunchtime Monday," Mrs. B said to Ophelia. "You'll report to the library conference room to get some anti-bullying work done. Are we clear?"

"*Sí*," Ophelia said.

She didn't even look that upset over being called a bully. I was so glad I had the Stone Face to use because I had no acting skills at all.

Over the weekend, when I wasn't eating outside with Dad and Jackson—because Jackson said if one of *us* sat still for too long Dad would put us on his new grill—or doing house chores or homework, I was studying my Five-Step Plan.

That was what was in the envelope I got sixth period, that practically started a catfight between Ophelia and Kylie. Lydia had typed it out in fancy writing:

STEP ONE: *Find a one-line assertive response for bullies.*
STEP TWO: *Even though bullying is not your fault, you can still do things to avoid being a target.*
STEP THREE: *Find a place for yourself so you're better able to deal with those who don't have a place for you.*
STEP FOUR: *Stop blaming God and look at what God can do.*
STEP FIVE: *Love your enemies.*

I didn't understand Step One, but I was sure Lydia would help me with that. I liked the sound of Steps Two and Three; I might be able to do those. Step Four could be hard. Really hard. So hard I didn't want to think about it yet.

Step Five, though? That was never going to happen. The whole idea of loving Kylie Steppe made me want to climb up the walls of my room.

By Saturday night, though, I had talked myself off the ceiling. Steps Four and Five were probably a long way off. I should probably just get started on the first three. *Baby Steps.* Lunch with Lydia couldn't come fast enough.

But there was Sunday to get through. Dad took us to church as usual. Well, *dragged* is a better word. The first time I whined about it to Jackson, he said Dad was "totally into God," so I should just shut up and deal with it. Like *he* did. He did his best sulking in church.

I didn't used to mind that much. I liked the music and some-times the sermon when the pastor told a joke or a story. Mostly, I used to like sitting next to my dad. When did I ever get him for a whole hour? Even though he obviously wasn't thinking about me, I could pretend he liked being there with me.

But that stopped about a year before we moved to Grass Valley, when we were in the town before Fresno, which was Stockton. The preacher there was fun to watch because he got all into what he was talking about and, well, talk about a bullhorn. He had "passion," Dad said, which I decided meant he really believed what he was saying. So he must have really, really believed what came out of him one Sunday when he said that God could do anything God wanted. He *chose* to let His people suffer sometimes so they would come to Him.

I almost stood up right on the pew and shouted, "Who wants a God like that?"

I didn't, of course, but ever since then, I hated going to church. I couldn't talk to God if He *chose* not to save my mom, and He *chose* to let things be so hard for our family since we didn't have her salary as a nurse now or her hugs or any of the other things I could barely remember anymore.

I went to church without whining though because I didn't want to upset my dad, especially now. But I didn't have to speak to God.

Usually during the sermon, I tried to make up new scenes in my head for my fantasy story, which was, like, six books long in there already. But that day, Sunday, March 22, something kept bugging me.

STEP FOUR: *Stop blaming God and look at what God can do.*

That didn't make any sense. How could I *not* blame God if God was the one who decided my mom had to be taken from us in the first place?

I know what You can do, I thought. *You can let people die in accidents that must have been so awful the kids can't even be told. So horrible other people can use it to keep me away from my friends. Why did you choose to give me friends and then take them away? It doesn't make sense, God!*

"Let us pray," the pastor said.

Wait.

I *was* praying. How did that even happen?

After the service, I stood in the back of the church while Dad shook hands with everybody in the whole place and Jackson went out to wait in the van. I'd been talking to God, all right, but was that the way you were *supposed* to do it? All getting up in His face?

"Hi."

I looked up. Colin was standing there. His hair was damp, and he had on a shirt that buttoned and jeans that were brand-new stiff.

"You're here!" I said.

"So are you," he said. "Go figure, huh?"

"Yeah."

Even though it was crazy seeing him someplace besides school, I suddenly wanted to ask him how he prayed. He never blinked at anything else I asked him . . . But then Dad called to me from the door, so I didn't.

"So, bye," Colin said.

"Yeah. See you tomorrow?"

"Definitely."

He was walking backward. Two more steps and he'd collide with the rack of booklets about Lent.

I started to warn him, but I was too late.

Brochures splashed to the floor. Colin's foot got caught in the rack, and he couldn't kick it off.

"Ginger, let's go," Dad said near my ear. "Don't embarrass the poor kid."

Too late for that too. My own face felt like a hot blotchy mess, so I could imagine what was going on with Colin.

It was sort of like I'd just seen the male version of myself.

Chapter Eight

I thought Monday couldn't come soon enough. But when we got to P.E., I decided it had gotten there *too* fast. We lined up in our teams, and Coach announced we were going to start the wall climb.

Why, oh, why couldn't I get small pox or all of a sudden discover I had a broken arm or have an asthma attack (even though I didn't have asthma)? I had been dreading this for eleven days, and now all that fear gathered in my stomach and I wanted to double over. It was real pain. Why didn't that disqualify me from the wall climb?

"This is how we're going to do this, people," Coach barked. Like a pit bull.

I heard Winnie give a little cry all the way over in the other line. She was probably wishing for small pox too.

"You'll go up two at a time, one person from each team. Alternating the boys' teams and the girls' teams. Clear?"

He didn't wait for any of us to go, "Huh?"

"You see we have mats in case you slip and fall."

He kicked at the mini-mattresses on the ground at the bottom of the wall. They didn't look thick enough to me.

"You'll also have us as spotters watching you."

Watching me break my neck?

"Iann! Demonstrate."

Mitch stepped out of our line and stood in front of the wall, staring up.

"Notice that she assesses the situation before she starts."

I already had. It was too hard.

Coach continued to tell us what Mitch was doing as, big as she was, she went up the wall like Spider-Man. She was back on the ground before I realized I hadn't really heard any of the instructions. I was sure even the bottoms of my feet were blotchy.

Tori and Kylie were the first pair of girls to go. Those Girls screamed for Kylie, while Tori's team jumped up and down going, "You got this, Tori! Go!" I was afraid to cheer for one team and refused to cheer for the other.

Tori won, and her team went nuts. I tried to swallow the miserable glob in my throat, but my stomach wasn't having it.

Two boys went next, then two more girls . . . until the only pair left was Winnie and me.

I was paralyzed. Seriously. I could not move.

"You can so do this," said a husky voice in my ear.

Mitch saying that was the only reason I went to the wall. And the fact that Winnie was obviously as terrified as I was made me reach up, find a place to put my hands, and then fumble my foot around until it landed on something below. I had never seen Winnie so pale.

She looked over at me, and I nodded at her. She nodded back and closed her eyes.

"It isn't gonna happen *that* way!" Coach barked. "If you two go any faster, you'll actually start moving!"

I tried to force myself to reach higher, but my hand wouldn't budge.

"Left hand straight up!" I heard Mitch yell.

I tried that. My hand landed on something, but my palm was so sweaty, it slipped. Panicked, I clung to whatever I could, but it all slid out from under me and I landed on my back on the mat. The sky spun above me.

"Get up!" girls were screaming.

All but Mitch. I heard her husky voice yell, "You can't do it either, Winnie, so you might as well quit now!"

I sat straight up on the mat and stared at Mitch. I couldn't look at Winnie. I knew she'd be dripping down the wall like rain. Mitch actually *said* that to her?

Evidently so, because Coach jabbed his finger at Mitch and his neck veins bulged like ropes. "To the office, Iann!" he screamed at her.

"Hey." Mrs. Zabriski left Winnie clinging to the wall about four feet up and hurried over to Coach. "We're supposed to send bullies to that lunchtime lady, remember?"

"Whatever." Coach's eyebrows did that hood thing. "Iann, you're doing that lunch thingy in the library. And a zero for the day. Now, all of you, hit the locker rooms!"

The whole class bolted like they couldn't wait to get inside; I trailed along behind. Whatever was going on, I couldn't get involved in it. But what was happening? First, Ophelia in Spanish class Friday, and now Mitch? I should start a new list: *Things That Don't Make Any Sense to Me.*

Second period was like an enormous beehive with everyone buzzing. I kept my head down and my Stone Face on.

In third period, Mrs. Collier-Callahan had us doing equations on the board. When Tori went up there, I got ready to copy down whatever she did. She was the smartest girl in that class. But when Mrs. C-C gave her $x + 3 = 6$, she wrote $3 = 6 - x$. Then she erased it and put $3 = x - 6$.

At that point, Winnie started giggling. It wasn't the silver bell I thought was so pretty. It was an I'm-making-fun-of-you laugh that didn't sound like Winnie and just didn't stop, even after Mrs. C-C gave her one of those looks that made you feel like she was shooting nails out of her eyes.

Tori turned from the board, one hand on her hip.

"She's making me feel awful," she said.

Actually, in that wooden voice, she could have been saying, "She's making me a smoothie," but Mrs. C-C snapped her fingers at Winnie.

"That's unkind, Winnie, and I'm surprised at you. I think you need a little tune-up. Report to the library at lunch."

Winnie ducked her head and nodded. I waited for her to burst into tears, but what I heard instead was Tori saying, "Ha-ha." Kind of like kids did on playgrounds in first grade.

"Honestly!" Mrs. C-C said. "Is there a full moon?"

I didn't know what that had to do with it, but something was definitely really wrong.

"This isn't a punishment, ladies," Mrs. C-C said as she filled out a slip at her desk. "When you act that way, something is going on with you and you may need some help figuring out what that is. Although—I have to say I'm a bit confused."

I was too. I glanced at Kylie, and I thought her face was what you call *smug*.

I guess I was what you call *slow* because it didn't dawn on me until we were all gathered in the conference room in the library with Lydia—Tori, Mitch, Ophelia, Winnie, and me—that they'd done it on purpose. It had taken me all morning to figure it out. It took Lydia about five seconds.

"Did you do what I think you did?" she said. She was smileless.

"We had to talk to you," Tori said to me. "And we couldn't figure out any other way."

"You took a hit for the team, I'll give you that," Lydia said. "But there will be no more of this, do you understand? You're the leaders of this movement. If you mess around with it, everybody will think it's just a joke."

"Sorry," Ophelia said. She was already taking the end of her braid to her mouth. "But as long as we're here"—she turned to me—"can we talk, please?"

There was nothing more in the whole world I wanted to do. Why couldn't I? Here in this secret room with nobody else listening? Where Lydia said whatever was shared in here stayed in here?

I even opened my mouth. But my next thought was, then what? It couldn't change what would happen outside the room. If I hung out with them, there wouldn't just be rumors on Twitter. *Everybody* would know what Those Girls were saying, and it wouldn't matter if it was true or not. It would hurt my dad so bad. And my brother. And me.

"I can't," I said.

"Why?" Ophelia said.

"Ladies." Lydia put her tiny hand up. "If Ginger isn't ready to talk, we shouldn't force her. Why don't we all have a seat and make the best of the time we have?"

Everyone found a chair around the table. There were no snacks, and it sure wasn't Tori's kitchen, but that wasn't the only thing that made it seem all different and wrong.

"It's clear to me," Lydia said, "that Kylie's bullying days are not yet over. She's just gone underground."

I tried not to gasp out loud. Did she know about the Twitter thing? And the e-mail to me?

But she went on. "So I think Step One in the Five-Step Plan Ginger's using applies to all of us."

She nodded at me. I didn't have to look at the sheet because I had them memorized.

"Find a one-line assertive response to bullies."

"I don't know what that means," Ophelia said.

Mitch grunted.

My stomach ached.

"Assertive," Lydia said, "means you know who you are and you don't let anyone take that away from you."

"So it's not power over, it's power to," Tori said.

"Just like you taught us," Winnie said.

"Right. So a one-line assertive response is a sentence you have at the ready that shows that."

"Example," Mitch said.

"Here's mine when someone says something snarky about my size." Lydia straightened up in the chair. "'It's all about what I do with what I've been given.'"

"Oh," Tori said. "I think I get it. Mine's 'I'm geeked out and proud of it.'"

"You said that to Kylie!" I said.

Lydia tilted her head. "And what happened?"

Tori blinked. "Nothing. She dropped it."

"Exactly," Lydia said.

"I got mine," Mitch said. "It's 'Wow.'"

"That's it?" Winnie said.

"Yeah. Somebody puts me down, I go, 'Wow.' What are they gonna say, right?"

Lydia grinned. "We'll work on that. Anybody else?"

It took all of lunch, but Ophelia found hers: "You definitely have a right to your opinion." And so did Winnie: "I like being me."

I, of course, was the only person who didn't discover one. Lydia said that was okay. It would come to me.

"Will you tell us what it is when you find it?" Tori said when the bell rang to end lunch.

Yes! I wanted to say. But how? I shrugged, and as I watched them all leave the library with Tori looking back once at me, I felt like I'd lost absolutely everything.

"Are you sure about this, Ginger?" Lydia said.

"No," I said. "But I don't have a choice."

I felt a small hand on my shoulder.

"Oh, my friend," she said. "You always have a choice."

Maybe it was the sudden sending of people to Lydia that stopped the bullying on Tuesday. Or maybe it was because Winnie, Tori, and Ophelia insisted on apologizing to the classes they "bullied" in. Mitch wanted to do it in P.E., but Coach said that was a waste of time, so she did it in the locker room, standing up on a bench. Just about everybody listened.

But people obviously hadn't forgotten about the Twitter rumor. They weren't saying anything to me, probably because they didn't want to give up their lunch freedom, but the slitty eyes that said *Your mom got in a car with a drunk driver? Who does that?* and the scrunched foreheads that called out to me *We've known about drunk driving since we were, like, seven. Was your mom clueless?* and the folded lips that shouted *You must be just like your mom, then, right?* was all still there. It was so loud I could hardly hear Lydia's voice in my head: *You always have a choice.* If she knew the whole story, would she still say that?

One thing did help me quiet all of it down, and that was trying to think of my one-line assertive response, just in case somebody did say one of those things—or worse—out loud. I started a list, but they all made me want to stick a label that said *Lame* right in the middle of my forehead.

You don't even know anything about it. That was fighting back.

Yeah, well, your mom's so skinny, Kylie, she's probably anorexic. That was turning into a bully myself.

Nothing you say can hurt me. That wasn't even true. Lydia even said it to us once. *Sticks and stones can break my bones, but words can break my heart.*

I wasn't any closer to a one-liner when I got to fifth period on Tuesday, and I didn't have time to think about it then because Colin and I were on Step Three: *Discover what the story is about and state it in one sentence.*

"So, it's not the plot," Colin said as we sat with our copies of *The Lord of the Rings* open and our chins in our hands. "That's Frodo trying to get the Ring to Mordor so he can destroy it. We have to figure out what the *story* is."

"I don't have a clue," I said. Which had to mean I wasn't as smart as I thought I was.

"I don't either," Colin said.

"May I offer some assistance?"

I just about bobbed my head off as Mr. Devon sat down across from us. He was rubbing his hands together again, like the next few moments were going to be delicious.

"Who is our protagonist?" he said.

"Is that the same as the main character?" I said.

"Correct."

"Frodo," Colin said. "Right?"

"Some would argue, but I happen to agree." Mr. Devon pressed his hand flat against his chest. "And what does Frodo learn from his journey?"

"That all who wander are not lost?" Colin said.

My all-time fave quote. If I had been Mitch, I would have high-fived him. She always used to do that with me.

"Can you dig deeper?" Mr. Devon said.

I closed my eyes and tried to see Frodo as he stood with the Ring in his hand, not being able to let go of it because the evil was getting power over him. I held back a cry as I watched Sam do it for him. That scene always made my heart hurt.

"One person can't destroy the power of evil alone?" I said.

"Brilliant!" Mr. Devon said.

Colin gave me the whole smile. "*Totally* brilliant."

"That's the right answer?" I said.

"It's *your* answer," Mr. Devon said, "and in my opinion you ought to run with it."

He gave us a silent clap and slipped off to deal with some kids who were making noise at another table. Armpit noise, to be exact. I looked at Colin, who was writing on the big piece of paper we'd been brainstorming on. He really was different. Right now, he was the only kid I could even talk to. But . . .

I turned my face away. He only hung out with me at lunch because of the project. When it was done April 14, he'd be gone and I'd be alone again.

"You okay?" he said.

When I looked back at him, I realized my eyes were blurry.

"Allergies?" he said.

"No," I said, because I was tired of not telling the whole truth. "I'm sad."

Colin nodded back his silky hair. "Yeah. I feel that way a lot. I know this sounds weird, but I think I'm Frodo sometimes. Not for real, but, you know."

"I do," I said.

His face was going pink, and I was on Blotch Number One. We both looked at the big piece of paper and talked at the same time.

"Now we have to do Step Four . . . is this like applying it to us? This is epic . . . we could start with . . ."

Colin did the halfway grin and pointed at me. "You go first."

I put my hand to my neck and felt the blotch cool. "It's like I'm living this all the time. I got bullied, and I had friends who helped me. And then the bullies made it so I can't be with my friends, and I want to fight the bullying, but I'm by myself again." I had to swallow down tears. "And now I really know I can't do it alone."

Colin was staring at the paper, not saying anything.

"I guess that's just a girl thing," I said. "Don't boys just pound each other and it's over? That's what Coach said. Not that I believe everything he says."

"He doesn't know what he's talking about." Colin's voice broke off at the end of his words like it sometimes did. "I've never gotten hit or anything. I just have to listen to them call me a Freak and a Geek and say I'm gay."

"But you ignore it," I said.

"That doesn't mean I don't hear it."

I nodded into the quiet. "Don't you want to tie their tongues in a knot sometimes?"

He half smiled. "That's good. I guess I do. The only thing is . . . well, this is what Mr. Devon told me: I'm master of my own tongue, not theirs."

Something shifted inside me, like an old thing was being shoved aside by a new thing.

"Will you say that again?"

"What?"

"That part about your tongue."

"I'm master of my own tongue, not theirs," Colin said.

"Could I borrow that?"

"Yeah. But what for?"

"A one-line assertive response."

Colin moved his lips as if he were trying that out on his mind. Then he wrote on the paper and said, "You'd have to say it this way."

In purple marker he'd written, *I am mistress of my own tongue, not yours.*

"I love it. So. Much," I said.

"Hey," Colin said.

"What?"

"I think we just came up with our life lesson."

"You mean, like, we can't stop the evil of bullying by ourselves."

"Yeah. And we can't change the bullies themselves. I mean, right? Sauron didn't change. Or Morgoth."

"Sam and Frodo just had to get past everybody."

Colin's face got serious, and he looked at me, totally without turning red.

"This *is* going to be epic," he said.

I believed him. And that felt good. Even if it might only be until April 14.

Jackson didn't walk home four feet behind me that afternoon. In fact, he somehow got there before I did and was already in his cave with the door shut. He'd put a sign on it that said: *Don't Even Knock. I Don't Want To Talk.*

How could we be brother and sister and be so different? He almost never wanted to talk about stuff, and I *always* wanted to, whether there was anything to really say or not. Of course, now that I knew I was mistress of my own tongue, I might not have to be wagging it all the time.

Still, I felt lonely, and I practically knocked Dad over when he came in the front door from work. I wrapped my arms around his waist and buried my head in his shirt and squeezed.

"You okay?" Dad said.

"I'm just glad to see you."

"Glad to see you too, but I'm all sweaty and dirty."

"I don't care," I said. But I let go because I knew he wanted me to. Hugging was hard for him.

"You do your homework?" Dad said as I followed him into the kitchen.

"Yes, sir."

Dad stopped, hand on the lunch box he was setting on the counter. "When did you start calling me 'sir'?"

"Today," I said.

"Huh. Where's your brother?"

"In his room."

"Go tell him dinner's ready in fifteen. I'm too tired to cook. You mind frozen pizza?"

Actually, I kind of wanted hummus and pita and baby carrots. I didn't say that, of course. What I did say was, "Do I have to talk to Jackson?"

"Yes."

"He's in a bad mood."

"So, what else is new?" Dad said into the freezer.

"No, *really* bad."

"Just knock on his door and tell him I said to be at the table in fifteen minutes."

"But there's a sign—"

"Ginger." Dad closed his eyes. "Can't handle this tonight. Just do it."

Okay, so I had to. But I wasn't going to be responsible for the big meltdown that was about to happen. Jackson would say, *Can't you read?* and I would say, *Can't you hear?* and then he would say . . .

I stopped in front of his door. I did know what Jackson was going to say, and whatever *I* said wasn't going to stop him. Was this what it meant? My one-liner?

I didn't knock because the sign said not to. And I wasn't going to make him talk either.

"Jackson?" I said. "Dad says dinner's in fifteen minutes."

"Tell him I'm not hungry."

"You tell him."

"Come on, just tell him I'm sick and I can't eat."

"Sorry," I said. "I'm mistress of my own tongue, not yours."

He was quiet, and I'd just about decided to run back to the kitchen before he could call me Freak Show when the door opened a crack. I could only make out Jackson's left eye. His swollen, purple left eye. Actually, all I could really see were his eyelashes and a glob of puffed-up skin that looked like an ape's behind.

"What—"

"Shhhhhh!"

I put my hand over my mouth and bit into one of my fingers so I wouldn't scream.

"I can't come out yet," he said. "Dad'll freak if he sees it this bad."

I had to agree with him on that one.

"Tell him I'm sick and I'll owe you."

"Okay," I whispered.

The door closed, and I heard it lock. I waited until I was sure I wasn't going to throw up before I went to Dad.

"He coming?" Dad said.

"No. He's . . . got issues."

"Issues? What does that mean?"

"Body issues. He really feels bad. He just wants to rest."

So far, I was telling the truth. Now all I could do was hold my breath.

"You can take him something later," Dad said finally. "Let's you and me eat."

When he turned to get the pizza out of the oven, I saw that his back was sort of bent and he was moving way slow.

For the first time ever, I was glad he was too tired to talk.

Chapter Nine

I had a nightmare that night. That used to happen all the time until a few weeks ago. This one was full of me being chased by a guy whose whole face looked like the back end of a baboon. He was coming after me in a car that swerved all over the road, and all these people in Mr. Potato Head masks and Barbie doll heads were screaming for me to stop him. I kept running until I came to a wall, and the only way to escape was to climb over it. But I couldn't.

When I woke up, I practically had to wring the sweat out of my pajama T-shirt, and my head was pounding like Dad was in there banging one of his big hammers. I couldn't eat any breakfast, and I didn't bother to pack a lunch because my stomachache was as bad as my headache. I couldn't even count the times that had happened to me, or the times I'd gotten Dad to let me not go to school.

But Jackson was obviously staying home, and I kind of didn't want to be there alone with him. His swollen-up face scared me. And *why* he had it scared me even more.

Boys who were involved in bullying got pounded, Coach said. I hoped Colin was right when he said Coach didn't know what he was talking about.

So I dragged myself to school with my head trying to split open and my stomach so full of tight knots I could hardly stand up straight. On the way with my umbrella, I did thank God that it was raining. That meant we wouldn't do the wall climb.

I remained mistress of my own tongue all morning, as in I didn't talk at all, not even at first when Colin sat with me at lunch and pulled out our folder of ideas.

"I was thinking about this last night," he said.

I nodded.

"Where's your lunch?"

"You were thinking about my lunch last night?"

"Are you okay?" Colin searched all over my face. "No offense, but you look sick."

"I kind of am."

"Is it about your brother getting in a fight?"

My mouth fell open in slow motion.

"Your brother's Jackson, right?" Colin said.

I could only nod again. My mind hadn't caught up yet.

"My brother's in his classes." Colin pushed his sandwich aside so he could lean both arms on the table. I leaned, too, to hear him over the cafeteria chaos.

"He told me some kids in seventh are spreading a rumor about . . . some stuff."

He suddenly looked like the sandwich had gone down wrong, and he couldn't seem to look at me.

"About what?" I said. "About my mom's accident?"

"Yeah."

"I want to know what they're saying."

Colin shook his head.

"Okay, I don't *want* to know, but I have to. Please?"

Colin shrugged until his shoulders went past his ears. "They're saying your dad got drunk and drove the car, and that's how your mom got killed."

I covered my face with both hands.

"Aw, man. I shouldn'ta told you."

"It's not true," I said through my fingers.

"Okay—"

"I was *with* my dad and Jackson when we got the phone call that she was in an accident."

This could *not* be happening. I did everything Those Girls said and it didn't matter. They still spread lies. To everyone. Even Jackson.

I pulled my hands down. Colin was as pink as one of Those Girls' backpacks, and he looked as miserable as I felt.

"Sorry," he said.

"Tell me everything," I said. "How did the fight start?"

Colin shook his knees back and forth under the table, vibrating the whole thing. "My brother has sixth-period P.E. with him, and some guy said that about your dad to Jackson's face. Jackson jumped him, and they got into it in the locker room. The other guy had a bloody nose, and your brother's eye, like, swelled up and he just left school."

"He cut sixth period?"

"My brother told Coach that Jackson went to the nurse. He never checks that stuff."

"Okay," I said. "Colin?"

"Yeah?"

"I'm going to be sick."

I just made it to the girls' restroom. When I came out, I went to the nurse. She called Dad and sent me home.

Jackson was on the couch when I got there. He had a bag of frozen peas on his face, and he was watching TV with his other eye.

"What are you doing here?" he said without looking away from the old Batman cartoon.

"I heard what happened to you and I got sick."

Yeah, not only did he turn from the TV . . . he switched it off. "It's not your problem," he said. "I ended it. It's over."

"No, it's not," I said. "It's just starting."

Jackson rolled his good eye and sat up on the couch. A paper plate that smelled like pepperoni turned over on the floor. "Look, don't go all drama queen," he said. "I got it handled."

"You don't understand—"

"Let it die!"

"Jackson . . ."

I stopped myself this time, because I heard Dad's van pull into the driveway.

"Go!" I said.

"Go where?" Jackson said.

"To your room. So Dad doesn't see!"

The front door opened, but Jackson just sat there.

"What's going on?" Dad said.

His hair and shoulders were sprinkled with sawdust, which he didn't brush off as he left the door open and came over to us. His boots left perfect mud footprints on the wood floor.

He looked at me first. "School said you were sick. What's wrong?"

"I have a headache and a stomachache." And a broken heart. But I didn't say that part.

"Now I got two of you down."

He turned to Jackson, and I considered running to my room and heading for the closet. But this whole thing was my fault. I couldn't just leave Jackson here by himself when Dad finally realized he had gorilla buns for a face.

"What the Sam Hill?" Dad said.

"I got in a fight," Jackson said. Just like that. Just like he was saying, "I got a B in math."

"I guess you did. Let me see that."

"It's fine," Jackson said.

But he moved the ice bag, and even though it looked better than it did last night, Dad whistled as he studied the purple mess.

He straightened back up. "This happen yesterday?"

"Yeah."

"You didn't tell me."

"I had to think about it."

"You get in trouble at school for it?"

"No."

"What does the other guy look like?"

Was Dad actually about to *smile?*

"Bloody nose. One guy e-mailed me and said it wasn't broken."

"Probably for the best. Just keep ice on it."

Jackson plopped the bag of peas back on his face and reached for the remote. Dad turned to me. I was one big blotch, and I didn't even bother to close my mouth.

"I know what your lady is telling you," he said. "But eventually you're going to have to fight back." He jerked his thumb toward Jackson. "I don't mean get in a fistfight. But you have to stand up for yourself. That's it. Bottom line."

"I have to go lie down," I said.

"Okay." Dad's face got softer. "You need anything?"

I didn't answer. But when I got almost to my room, I came back.

"Her name is Lydia," I said.

"What?"

"My lady. Her name is Lydia. She's telling me the truth. And she's about the only one who is."

I ran to my room. Just before I slammed the door, I heard Dad say to Jackson, "I just don't know what to do with a girl."

"Who does?" Jackson said.

All I could do until lunch the next day was count the minutes before I could see Lydia. She had lunch ready for us again—soup with all kinds of veggies in it. My stomach still hurt, but I ate some because I hadn't put any food in it since . . . I couldn't exactly remember.

Lydia waited until I pushed the half-full bowl away before she said, "Do you want to tell me about it?"

I wasn't sure what I could say. *Tell me what truth you can,* she said that first day. So I did. Very carefully.

"My brother got in a fight because of something I told Kylie that got all . . . blown up."

"Is he okay?"

"Yeah. And my dad thinks he's all wonderful because he fought back."

"Can you control that?" Lydia said.

The question surprised me, but I had to shake my head.

"Let's look at what you *can* control."

"Not my mouth, obviously. It's like when I'm around Kylie, stuff comes out of it that I know I shouldn't have said before I'm even done saying it. Like the thing that started the rumor that my dad can*not* find out about."

"I see." Lydia tapped her lips. "I have an idea, but I want to make sure you understand something first."

"Okay," I said.

"The bullying that happens to you is not your fault. You can, however, do some things to avoid being a target."

"Like the Stone Face," I said.

"Yes. Be clear, though: we're going to change how you respond, but we're not going to change the true you. I'm not going to say, 'Change yourself and they'll leave you alone.'" She tilted her head. "Make sense?"

"Sort of."

"Maybe an example will help. Things come out of your mouth before you think about them."

"Yes."

"What if you tried to make it a habit to write down what you want to say to Kylie or her followers? You can look at it and see if you really want to say it. That slows everything down and gives you a chance to think about it."

"Where do I write it?"

Lydia held up a finger for me to wait while she dug around in the red canvas bag. She pulled out a little notebook. It was like the spiral ones we used in science lab, only smaller. Lydia stuck a blue gel pen in the rings and handed me the whole thing.

"A gift for you," she said.

"Thank you!" I held it in my hand like it was the Ring itself, only in a good way. "This goes along with my one-liner," I said. "I forgot to tell it to you."

"I want to hear."

Lydia folded her miniature hands under her chin and looked into me like my eyes were deep pools she was trying to see into, and I almost started to cry.

"'I'm mistress of my own tongue, not yours,'" I said. "Colin helped me with it."

"And who is Colin?"

"A boy I know."

The blotching started, but Lydia didn't wink or go "ooh" or anything else that looked like, *Isn't that precious? She thinks she has a boyfriend.* I loved her so much.

"Anything else you feel comfortable telling me?" she said.

I shook my head. She looked at me for a minute longer—which she did a lot, actually—and stuck her hand in the bag again. This time she pulled out the sticky notes and the green marker.

"More labels?" I said.

"This time we're going to make the ones you put on yourself."

"Oh." I didn't have to think about it that much. "Klutz. I totally am. You should see me trying to climb the wall in P.E. every day."

"You don't have to defend them." Lydia stuck the *Klutz* label on me. "What else?"

"*Smushy.*"

"Smushy."

"Not really fat, but not, like, thin as a pencil."

"Got it. Go on."

"*Smart But Stupid-Looking. Blabbermouth.*"

I was on a roll. Lydia had to write fast to keep up with *Different, Not Pretty, Too Dramatic,* and *Hypochondriac.*

Lydia lifted her eyebrow at that last one.

"My dad took me to the doctor when I first started having headaches and stomachaches, and the doctor couldn't find anything wrong with me. I wasn't supposed to be listening, but I heard my dad ask him if I was a hypochondriac, and I asked Jackson what it meant. He said it's where you think you're sick when you're really not because you're a crazy person."

Lydia closed her eyes for a few seconds. When she opened them, she said, "Since that's a label someone else put on you, what do you say we leave it out?"

I looked down at my T-shirt, which was covered in yellow squares again. "I don't think there's room for any more."

"So it looks like you bully yourself as much as everybody else does," Lydia said. "Our next step—"

She didn't get to finish because the door was shoved open, and it banged against the inside wall of the conference room. Heidi came in with a face the color of Lydia's bag. She was breathing like she just ran laps for Coach. Like he would ever make *her* do that.

"Hey there," Lydia said. "We're having a meeting—"

"I *know*," Heidi said with an eye roll in her voice. "I'm supposed to be here."

"Are you sure?" Lydia said.

"Mr. Jett sent me. He said I was being ugly to someone in the lunchroom."

How was that different from any other day?

"Let's start with your name then," Lydia said.

"I'm Heidi," she said, like Lydia should have known that.

"And exactly what went down in the lunchroom that caused Mr. Jett to send you here, Heidi?"

Heidi didn't answer. She was staring at me. Me with my squares announcing that I was a smushy, stupid-looking, annoying, dramatic, blabbermouth of a person.

As if that was news to her.

She covered her mouth with both of her hands, but I saw the snorty laughter in her eyes. The kind of laughter you don't laugh along with because it's meant to stab you in the stomach. Which was what was happening that very minute.

"We're almost through with our session, Heidi." Lydia jerked the curls toward the door. "Mr. Jett will have to reschedule you."

"Okay!" Heidi said.

She bolted from the room, and I knew it would only be a matter of minutes before Kylie and Those Girls knew I was in here pretending to be a bulletin board.

When Lydia turned back to me, I was already ripping the labels off.

"I'm sorry that happened," Lydia said. "How are you going to handle it next period?"

"Does it even matter?" I said.

"I think it does."

I plunked myself into my chair with the sticky notes wadded in my hand.

"What if they never stop?"

"What if you let them keep getting to you?" Lydia put her hand up. "The steps work, Ginger. But not overnight. Do you trust me?"

I had to nod.

"Then give it a go. What will you do?"

"Stone Face," I said.

"And?"

"Assertive response."

"Right. And?"

I looked at the sticky clump of paper in my hand. "Don't believe the labels?"

"Not even the ones you put on yourself." Lydia came close to me and looked into my eyes again, even deeper this time. "This should work. But something really disturbing is happening that you're not telling me about, and it's affecting your health. We can do all these things, but I can't stand by and watch that, Ginger. We're going to give it a few more days, but if we can't get results, I'm going to have to help you more than you seem to want me to."

"Because you have to."

"Because I want to. Because I love you."

I Saved the Tears until I got to the restroom, but I didn't cry. I stood in front of the mirror until I got my Stone Face on.

Assertive response at the ready, I told myself as I went to the Spanish room. Don't believe that you're a stupid bullhorn. Write it down before you say it.

When I got to my desk, I pulled out my special present from Lydia. Kylie appeared next to me, just as she had the other day. I put a protective hand over the notebook and pretended to focus on the assignment Mrs. Bernstein was writing on the dry-erase board.

"Ginger!" Kylie said.

I just looked at her.

"Heidi says that woman's class is *fascinating*." She leaned across the aisle, smiling the Barbie smile. "I wish you didn't have to act mean to get in there."

"Kylie."

We both looked up at Mrs. Bernstein. She was paused at the board with a black marker in her hand. The eyebrows were in a sharp *V*.

"What?" Kylie said.

"You're so much better than that."

She would have sent anybody else to Lydia's class. What did Kylie get? Practically nothing.

But when I looked over at Kylie, her eyes were stung, like she'd just been sentenced to a life of acne.

"Wow," I heard Mitch mutter.

It didn't last long, though. As we were passing our homework papers up to the front, Kylie looked over at me yet again.

"Can I ask you something?" she said.

"Sure," I said. "I'm mistress of my tongue, not yours."

I tried not to sound snarky. I didn't think I did. And Kylie didn't give me a snarky comeback. She just looked . . . surprised. I turned away before that could morph into something else.

"Let's get started on the assignment, *mis estudiantes*," Mrs. Bernstein said. "It's due at the beginning of the period tomorrow."

Good. I would do it for homework. Right now, I needed to get started on that new list: *Things I Decided Not To Say*. I began with the things I'd bitten back already, including what Kylie said first.

It took me until the end of the period. Maybe I wasn't so much of a blabbermouth after all. If only I hadn't blabbed that one important thing.

Chapter Ten

⁓

Something did change after that.

Part of it was in me. I was still scared about the things people were saying that I didn't hear. But whenever my stomach pinched in, I thought about Lydia saying this wasn't going to happen overnight. That usually a plan like ours worked. That I could trust her. I had to think about that or I couldn't eat. My gym sweats were falling off me.

Part of the change was in the air, and it wasn't just the warm spring. It was about even the molecules feeling tense the minute we got out to the obstacle course on Friday.

We were in full run-throughs, and I was doing a little better. Even though I always came in last, even behind Winnie, I could at least do everything, except the wall. We'd had so much rain the ground was thick and sticky and our tennis shoes made sucking sounds when we ran on it. Not only did we have to jump hurdles; we had to leap over puddles so deep you could've fished them.

I was the one most likely to fall into one, but as I rounded the bend in the circular course, right after the tunnel crawl and the sprint, I saw Tori go into one headfirst. And I saw how it happened. Izzy was crouched at the edge of the path like she was tying her shoe, and when Tori passed her, going way fast, Izzy just calmly stuck her leg out and Tori went flying and splashed into the mud.

I was the first one to get to her, but before I could even say, "Are you okay?" somebody pulled me back by the seat of my sweats and almost yanked them off me. I stopped to pull them up so I didn't expose my entire fanny to the BBAs, and by that time, Mitch was already helping Tori up.

"I got some extra sweats you can borrow," Mitch said.

"I have an extra pair too," Tori said. Which was good because she was, like, half Mitch's size.

"Take a shower, Taylor," Mrs. Zabriski called out. "You're done for the day."

When everyone went back to the course, I hung back and edged up to Mrs. Z.

"What is it, Hollingberry?" she said.

I felt like an annoying mosquito. And I so wasn't.

"Is Tori going to get marked down for today?" I said.

She shaded her eyes with her hand and watched the kids go for the hurdles. "Why is that your business?"

"Because if she is, I should tell you something."

"Not interested." She pulled her hand away from her eyebrows and looked at me. Her way-short hair didn't even move in the wind. "No, she's not getting marked down. Okay? Happy now?"

No, but I nodded and started back toward the course.

"Hollingberry," she said.

I turned and looked at her. If I'd had my notebook with me, I would have written, *What? I'm sick of you being on me all the time. I haven't done anything!*

"Have you lost weight?"

I thought about my loose sweats. "I guess so," I said.

"Are you eating healthy?"

"Sometimes." Like when Lydia fed me.

"Do it all the time. Eating disorders can start at this age. You don't want to get into that mess."

"Um, okay?"

She stuck her whistle in her mouth and blew before I had a chance to cover my ears. "All right, girls—back to the locker room."

I dragged my feet getting there so I could think about *that* scene. Mrs. Zabriski actually cared about my health? Smushy me?

By the time I got to the locker room, the tension was like a fog in there. A scene so dramatic it was Ophelia-worthy was already under way.

Kylie stood on the bench in our locker row, flipping her hair all over the place and whining, "It's gone! It's gone!"

"What is?" Tori said.

"My poem! For English!"

Those Girls gathered below her, looking up as if their queen were about to be dragged off to the executioner.

"Oh, no!" Heidi said. "It was so *good!*"

"You worked really hard on it," Riannon said.

"Yes, I did." Kylie ran her fingers through her hair the way I'd seen actors do in soap operas on days I stayed home sick. "I wrote, like, a whole epic about my best quality."

"Wow," Mitch said.

Ophelia turned away and literally stuck her whole head into her locker. I could see her shoulders shaking.

I would have laughed too. I mean, really, didn't Kylie hear what she just said? I didn't, though, because Kylie was staring hard at Tori.

"Where did you see it last?" Tori said, as if Kylie wasn't trying to drill holes into her with her eyes.

"It was in my backpack," she said.

"Was your backpack in your locker?" Tori said.

That was one of the things I liked best about Tori. She was so logical, even when everybody else was losing it.

"It wouldn't fit in my locker," Kylie said. "I just left it on the bench. I shouldn't have to lock all my things up."

Something to add to my list: *All your nice things you think everybody else wants?*

"Maybe you should look again," Tori said, just before she went back to combing the tangles out of her wet hair.

"I turned it upside down and dumped everything out. My poem. Is. Gone."

"I'm sorry that happened," Tori said.

Kylie stepped down from the bench and tossed her bob back. It was stringy from her dragging her hands through it, so it didn't toss so well.

"Someone else is going to be sorry, too, if I don't find it," she said.

Yeah, we could have scooped that tension up with a spoon. Something was building.

And speaking of poems, that day in fifth period, when Colin and I were putting our story ideas on index cards, Mrs. Fickus invaded the library with the whole class so they could find poems for their poetry notebooks and photocopy them. Mr. Devon couldn't be there for us because both he and his assistant had to be at the Xerox machine the whole time, or it would probably have been a disaster. BBAs working office equipment? That was scary.

I tried to concentrate on our story, but it was hard—especially with the Tribelet there working together, just like we'd all worked together on our science presentation just a few weeks before. Or was it a whole lifetime ago?

I was flipping through the ideas Colin and I had so far, and not actually soaking in what I was seeing, when Tori pulled a chair up next to mine.

"Could I talk to her for a minute?" she said to Colin.

Colin looked from her to me and I nodded and he went into the social sciences section. I couldn't help sending a panicky glance across the library where Those Girls were becoming hysterical over something the BBAs were showing them.

"This is school business," Tori said.

I didn't tell her that wouldn't make any difference to Kylie.

"We have to have somebody else read our poem and critique it before we turn it in," Tori said. "So, would you do mine?"

Kylie and Those Girls and anybody else who wanted to ruin my life drained away like I'd just flushed them down the toilet.

"You want *me* to do it?" I said.

"You're really good at it. You're doing this special project and everything."

I stared at the stack of cards, which were now practically melting in my hand. "I've sort of, like, shut you out. Aren't you mad at me?"

The laughter on the other side of the library stopped.

"We don't have time to talk about this now," Tori said in a low voice. She pushed a sheet of paper toward me. "Will you e-mail me what you think?"

"Do you need this back?" I said.

"I have another copy. Thanks."

After Tori disappeared into the crowd, I put the cards aside and read her poem. If I were Mitch, I would have said, "Wow."

I was sliding it carefully into my backpack when the mob suddenly seemed to expand. People were all around our table and reaching for books on the nearby shelves that weren't even poetry. In the middle of it, my backpack got knocked off and my stuff went everywhere. I heard Winnie shriek as her papers flew and got mixed up with mine. We were both on the floor on our hands and knees, along with Shelby and Colin and one of the soccer girls, when Mr. Devon finally called out:

"Silence! Let order be restored!"

Everybody got quiet for about three seconds, and then Riannon snickered and Patrick said, "Hey, dude, you talk weird."

Mrs. Fickus bustled over. She shooed Patrick away, and Mitch told everybody to get their feet off our papers. Mr. Devon said to Riannon, "I see you're amused, milady. Care to share?"

"No," she said.

I hoped Mr. Devon didn't hear her murmur, "What a freak." I really might have popped her one. Or something.

Order *was* finally restored, although people were still handing my stuff back to me at the end of the period. At least I had Tori's poem, and that was all I cared about.

It really was awesome, that poem. I read it for about the hundredth—okay, maybe the twentieth—time Saturday before I started the e-mail.

She wrote:

> *My hair is not the shiniest of bobs*
> *My eyes are not the brightest in the room*
> *My figure will not get me modeling jobs*
> *My smile will not bring young boys to their doom.*
> *But do I cry and mourn my average face?*
> *Or wish that I had boyfriends at the ready?*
> *Do I not sleep because I lose the race,*

Or spurn my food because I don't go steady?
My mind is on a more important thing
That lifts my heart and makes my spirit soar
I want to make the souls of people sing
And quiet down the mean and bullying roar.
To help the wounded girls replace the scar
With the right to be exactly who they are.

I wrote:

Dear Tori,
This is the most awesome poem ever, and I've read a lot of poems. The Lord of the Rings *is full of them. Also* The Hobbit. *But yours is better, and here's why:*

1. *It's a real sonnet. Fourteen lines of iambic pentameter and the right rhyme and everything. It's very professional.*
2. *It's supposed to be about your best quality and it is. You don't care what people think about the way you look, and you're not all boy crazy. You're about the important things like anti-bullying, and even though it seems like I don't appreciate your help, I do. I believe in everything you do. You're the leader, and I wish I could be like you.*
3. *It made me cry. Poems are supposed to get you to be emotional. I hardly ever cry over poems (I do over novels, though), but every time I read the last two lines in yours, I got big tears in my eyes. Once I even cried out loud. And now I feel better.*

I only have one criticism about your poem and it's this. The first four lines aren't exactly true. You are one of the cutest girls in our class, and when you smile, it makes people happy. Well, at least me.

Thank you for the honor of reading this poem. I know you'll get an A.

> *Sincerely,*
>
> *Virginia (Ginger) Eve Hollingberry*

I sent the e-mail and checked my inbox at least ten times for her answer. When she didn't write to me by Sunday night, I started to sink inside. I tried not to think of all the reasons that she wouldn't write me back: she thought it was a stupid critique, she didn't like the part where I told her some of it wasn't true even though I meant it as a compliment, she was mad at me for shutting her and the Tribelet out after all. But none of those fit the person in the poem. Tori wouldn't think any of those things.

My heart lifted (that was the way she described it in her poem) when she came up to me in the gym locker room before P.E. started. I didn't even look to see if Kylie was watching as Tori nudged me out the door to walk with her to the obstacle course.

"I don't get why you won't hang out with us," she said when we were outside. "But I'm trying to do like Lydia said and not bug you about it."

"Thanks," I said. My heart wasn't lifting anymore.

"But jeepers, Ginge." Her voice changed out of *I've been thinking about what to say* and into *I'm just going to come out with it.* "Do you have to be mean about it?"

"Mean?" I said.

"Yeah. Mean."

"Is someone being mean to you, Ginger?" Kylie said behind me.

I whipped around to face her. "I'm having a private conversation about school business," I said. So much for writing things down before I said them.

"You *were* having a private conversation," Kylie said, and smiled the smile that didn't even look like one.

I turned to find that Tori was gone.

The tension notched up again, and now some of it was coming from me. All morning I simmered like a pot of Dad's chili that was too hot for me to even eat.

I didn't know what Tori was talking about when she said I was mean, but it had to have something to do with Kylie. Me not being able to hang out with the Tribelet was one thing. But Tori getting her feelings hurt was a whole *other* thing.

That thing was, if Kylie and Those Girls were just hurting me, I wouldn't care so much. I could do the Stone Face and the one-liner and all the other things Lydia and the Tribelet had taught me, and it might go away like Lydia said.

But the harder I tried, the more *other* people got hurt, and for what? Wasn't the lie already all over the school that my dad caused my mom's accident by being drunk? Hadn't Jackson already found out and taken care of it himself by "pounding" some guy? What difference did it make now?

The difference was Dad, of course. If I could just find a way to tell him how it all got started, maybe he'd understand.

Or maybe he would go down into depression again and the house would get moldy and my grandmother would appear out of nowhere with papers from a judge.

One thing I did decide, though. I was going to talk to Lydia about it during lunch. I was going to tell her everything.

I was even writing stuff down at the end of third period so I wouldn't babble on like a moron when Mr. V came to my desk with a note.

"Special delivery for Ginger Hollingberry," he said, grinning his big elastic grin.

"Again?" I heard one of Those Girls say. They were all starting to sound alike to me.

I waited for everybody to stop looking at me before I unfolded it. *Please come to my room at the beginning of lunch,* it said, and it was signed, *Mrs. Fickus.*

She probably wanted to see how things were going with Mr. Devon. At least I had good news for *her.* Colin and I had our story almost outlined except for the big heroic scene and the end. I didn't like that this might cut into my time with Lydia, though.

So as soon as the bell rang, I rushed to the library, but she wasn't there yet, so I asked Mr. Devon to give her the message that I would be late.

"I think Mrs. Fickus wants to check our progress," I told him.

"Indeed?" he said. He looked a little confused, but I didn't have time to explain.

Mrs. Fickus just better be quick, I thought as I climbed back up the steps against the throng of kids going to the lunchroom. I needed all the time I could get to talk to Lydia.

But the minute I stepped into the English room, I hit a wall of tension higher than the one on the obstacle course. Mrs. Fickus was leaning on the front of her desk with her arms tightly folded and her rosy lips pulled in so hard her lipstick made angry feathers around her mouth.

This wasn't going to be a quick conversation.

Chapter Eleven

I wasn't the only one who had been . . . summoned, I think was the word for it.

Kylie was sitting in a desk in the front, looking kind of small and teary-eyed. I knew that look. I'd seen a version of it in the mirror plenty of times. She was acting like a victim, and in my opinion, she wasn't very good at it. How could she be? She didn't have any practice.

Tori sat next to her, and she wasn't acting at all. The fear in her eyes was totally real, and she was folding and unfolding her hands like she was totally distressed.

"Miss Hollingberry, have a seat, would you please?" Mrs. Fickus said.

I went to the other side of Tori and away from Kylie, who I didn't even look at again. Mrs. Fickus waited until I was still before she picked up two pieces of paper from the desk she was leaning on.

"Ginger," she said as she held them up like exhibits in a courtroom TV show, "I was just telling Miss Taylor and Miss Steppe that the poems they turned in are almost identical to each other. Kylie's is typed and Tori's is handwritten with some drawings, but other than that they are exactly alike. "

As quietly as I could, I pulled my little notebook out of the front pocket of my backpack and wrote down what I wanted to say, which was, *Kylie could NEVER write a poem like Tori's!*

Mrs. Fickus looked down her powdered nose. "Clearly we have a problem."

Kylie raised just her hand, not her whole arm, and gave Mrs. Fickus a simpering smile. You know, like one of the ugly stepsisters flirting with the prince.

Ophelia's right, I wrote. *You are the worst actress ever!*

"Yes, ma'am," Mrs. Fickus said to her.

"I can prove when I wrote mine." Kylie stuck her hand in her Pepto-Bismol pink backpack and pulled out something small. "It's on my jump drive, and when you pull it up, it'll show the last date I worked on it. Friday, March 27. That was after I . . . well, we don't need to talk about that."

She looked down at the desktop, all weepy and sweet. I was glad I hadn't eaten lunch yet.

But I didn't write that down. What I wrote was, *Tori gave me her poem fifth period on March 27.* When I looked up, Mrs. Fickus was watching me.

"Tori says you might be able to shed some light on this."

I could. But I really wanted to talk to Lydia first.

"Mrs. Fickus?" Kylie said.

"Yes, ma'am."

"There's one thing I didn't tell you."

"And that is?"

"My poem was missing for a while."

"What do you mean 'missing'?"

"First period Friday it wasn't in my backpack where I put it, and I didn't get it back until fifth period. It just showed up there again."

"So what makes you think it was ever missing? It could have been there all along."

"It wasn't! That's why I came in before school today to turn it in, before somebody stole it again."

Mrs. Fickus's cotton candy hair seemed to bristle. "There is no reason to believe it was stolen, Kylie."

"Yes, there is. Only, I didn't want to bring it up."

I scribbled, *Yes, you did! That's the whole reason we're here!*

My heart was trying to crawl up my throat. Kylie was really kind of scary. Okay, way scary. Scarier than I thought. As in, I would rather be pounded in the face than have to deal with the way she twisted things.

"All right," Mrs. Fickus said. Her voice was like a sigh. "What is your reason?"

"First period Friday, when my poem was in my backpack and not in my locker, Tori had to go into the locker room during P.E. class because she 'accidentally' fell in the mud and had to change."

No, I wrote furiously, *because one of your friends tripped her and made her fall.*

Mrs. Fickus turned to Tori. "In the interest of fairness, was *your* poem ever out of your possession?"

Yes, I wrote. *Friday fifth period after she gave it to me and those boys knocked over my backpack and papers went everywhere. You were THERE, Mrs. Fickus!*

I wanted to say it. I almost did. I wanted Tori to say it. But neither one of us had any more proof than Kylie did. I looked miserably at the things I'd just written down, wishing I could say all of them.

And then I saw it. At the top, where I'd written things I'd hadn't said to Kylie in the past, with her words first. *Isn't making a false accusation against your little Code?* she'd said to me.

I raised my hand. "Um, Mrs. Fickus, can I say something?"

"You absolutely can."

"I don't even see what Ginger has to do with this," Kylie said.

"You read Tori's poem, didn't you?" Mrs. Fickus said to me, as if Kylie hadn't even spoken.

"Yes," I said, "but this isn't about that . . . exactly."

"What *is* it about?"

Mrs. Fickus's patience was looking as thin as Kleenex. I had to talk fast.

"So, Kylie," I said, leaning out onto the desktop so I could see her. "One time you asked me if making a false accusation was against the Code and I didn't get to answer. But just so you know, it is. That's why I'm not saying when I think Tori's poem wasn't in my possession because it will sound like I'm accusing you. All I can say is that Tori gave me her poem to critique on Friday fifth period, and I e-mailed her Saturday and told her how good it was."

Tori looked at me like someone had just poked her with something sharp.

"Ginger has a point," Mrs. Fickus said.

The gold specks in Kylie's eyes flashed. "*I* don't think she has a point. Do teachers just let her get away with things because she doesn't have a mother and her father is a—"

"That is enough, Kylie." Mrs. Fickus stared her down until Kylie folded her arms and looked away. "Now, Tori, Kylie, I want you to go to opposite sides of the room and write down your poems. From memory."

"Not fair!" Kylie said.

"I think it is entirely fair," Mrs. Fickus said, "and if you don't stop arguing with me, I'm going to lower your citizenship grade two letters."

If I were ever going to see a person's head explode, this was the time.

But I was more worried about Tori's head. She moved to a desk on the other side of me, and she held her forehead in her hands and stared down at a blank sheet of paper.

"Don't let her do that to you," I whispered.

"She's totally helping her!" Kylie said.

Mrs. Fickus opened her laptop. "You're down to a B minus, Miss Steppe." But she nodded to me, and I went for the door. Just as I was stepping out into the hall, I looked back. Tori was writing. Kylie wasn't.

I leaned against the wall outside and closed my eyes and found myself praying for Tori. *Please choose to help her remember her poem.*

Although, even if she didn't, who would ever believe Kylie could write those things about herself? She would never say she didn't have the best hair or the brightest eyes.

"I can't do this! It's too much pressure!"

Kylie's voice came right through the brick wall like she was standing next to me. Before she could fly out of the room and actually be there, I fled for the library.

When I got to the conference room, there were turkey wraps on our table and Mr. Devon was having one with Lydia.

"Hey, there," Lydia said. "We saved one for you."

"I can't eat," I said.

Lydia pressed her hand on my shoulder until I sat in my chair. "What's going on?"

I had come in there to tell her everything, and I did—at least about what had just happened in Mrs. Fickus's room. I was all the way through it before I realized I had just spilled the whole thing in front of Mr. Devon. Wonderful. Now he was going to think I was a complete idiot to get myself into a mess like that.

But he was nodding, fingers rubbing his chin like an English detective. "It was madness in here fifth period Friday. That was the day we were photocopying poetry, and I completely lost control of the place."

"Someone could have copied Tori's poem and then gotten it back to you in the middle of it," Lydia said to me. "I think you should tell Mrs. Fickus that."

"But you said we shouldn't fight back."

"I said don't do to her what she does to you. But you can defend yourself or a friend against an accusation."

The door opened, like usual when something important was about to happen, and Mrs. Fickus came in. When I saw that she had my *Things I Decided Not To Say* notebook in her hand, I passed blotchy and went straight to bloodred. Scalp to toes, and I am not kidding.

"Sorry to interrupt y'all," Mrs. Fickus said. "But, Ginger, you left this in my classroom, honey."

I was *honey* again. Maybe she hadn't read it.

"I just glanced at it to see who it belonged to, and I couldn't help but see some of what you wrote." She glanced at Lydia and then looked back at me. "Something good is happening in this room, because you have tremendous self-control. Very impressive."

I couldn't even say anything.

"If you want to confront Kylie with this—"

"Could you just give Tori credit for the poem?" I blurted out. "We can't prove anything, so if you would just do that . . . that would be good and enough and, yeah, please do that."

"Done," Mrs. Fickus said. "And I'll have Kylie write a different poem." She cocked her head like a yellow-feathered bird. "I didn't think that sonnet sounded like her. Ms. Kiriakos, may I speak with you?"

"Absolutely," Lydia said, and she followed Mrs. Fickus out the door.

I looked down at my notebook. "I bet you hate girl drama, huh?" I said to Mr. Devon.

"What I dislike is deceit and manipulation."

"Me too."

Mr. Devon tilted his chin up at me. "And that, my dear, is what makes you a treasure of integrity."

Chapter Twelve

I took the dictionary to bed with me that night and looked up the word *integrity*. *Adherence to an ethical code*, it said.

I had to look up *adherence*, too, and it meant "sticking to".

I let the dictionary lay open on my chest and watched it go up and down as I breathed. Maybe that was true about me. We had a Code, and I stuck to it.

Or did I? The card I didn't use when I should have was *Report Alert*. If bullying got so out of hand somebody could get hurt, we were supposed to tell an adult. That was what I was trying to do fifth period, but the whole thing with Mrs. Fickus happened, and I didn't get a chance to talk to Lydia.

You are a treasure of integrity, Mr. Devon said.

He didn't know me that well, but at least the label he put on me sounded better than *Weirdo* and *Freak*.

I wanted to look up *treasure,* but I couldn't get my hands to move. They were too heavy. Maybe if I closed my eyes for just a few minutes, I could turn to the *T* section and find . . . whatever . . .

The next thing I knew a dog was barking and he didn't stop. I got my eyes open enough to see that the lamp beside my bed was off and a thin light was coming in between my curtains. The dog just kept on like he was about to become hysterical.

I climbed out of bed, and something hard hit the floor. Oh, yeah, the dictionary. It landed with its pages all crumpled underneath it, but I had to deal with yelling at the dog and closing my window first.

The barking went up into freak-out zone. I raised the window higher and opened my mouth to tell him to hush *up*, but I didn't. A car, maybe silver, was pulling away from the curb in front of our house and the tires squealed even louder than the border collie. It was too dark—and too surprising—for me to see who was inside, but as the dog chased it down the street, snarling at the tires, the red lights in back flashed on, and I saw a black circle on the trunk with another circle inside it, blue and white, and the letters *BM*—

The lights flashed off, and the silver car screeched toward the end of our street and was swallowed down the hill.

The dog strutted back to his house with his head all high. I closed the window, but I didn't go back to bed. Something bad had just happened; I could feel it in the tension wall that went up all around me. I would have just stood there, trapped in it, if I hadn't heard Dad going down the hall toward the living room, grumbling, "What the Sam Hill?"

I knew if he saw me, he would make me get back in my bed, so I tiptoed down the hall and out the front door, which he'd left hanging open. Dad was already in the yard, swinging a flashlight beam up in the trees like he was looking for more toilet paper. I crept after him as he continued on toward the driveway. He sniffed the air, and I did too. It smelled like his work clothes and our bathroom right after he painted it, only stronger.

I had to climb over the tension wall as I followed him. I came crashing down from it when I saw what he saw as he shined the flashlight on the other side of the van.

DRUNK DRIVER!

Someone had painted that in red letters right on top of *HOLLINGBERRY REMODELING.*

Dad's face turned the color of the ashes in our grill—I could see that even in the half dark. I could also see his mouth making a hard, sad line across his face. It looked like pain.

Me? I just screamed. I put my hands on my face to muffle it, but the sound still came, clawing its way up my throat on the way out, over and over. It kept on even when Dad put his arms around my waist and carried me inside with my feet banging against his legs.

When he got me to the couch, the screaming stopped and Jackson stumbled into the living room with his hair hanging in his face.

"What's going on?" he said.

"Vandalism," Dad said.

"Huh?"

"They painted 'Drunk Driver' on the van!" I said.

Jackson came awake fast, like I'd just slapped him. He bolted for the door and dodged as Dad tried to grab his arm. Then they were both outside, and there was yelling and shushing and stomping back up the front steps. Dad had his hand on Jackson's back when they came through the door.

"Tell me, Jackson," Dad said.

Jackson pulled away. "I said I don't know!"

"I think you do. *Does* this have anything to do with the fight you got into?"

Jackson's eyes were wild. He held out his arms. "How should I know? I don't even know who did it."

"Dad!" I said.

He stuck his hand up without looking at me because his eyes were so hard on Jackson, my brother backed into the TV stand.

"What would even put that idea into somebody's head?"

"People just start stuff up—"

"Dad!"

"It has to start from somewhere. Who said what to you when you punched that guy?"

"It was stupid . . ."

"What *was* it?"

"*Dad!*"

"Ginger, would you just back off? This has nothing to do with you." Dad's whole face blazed at me, but I still said, "Yes, it does."

"No." Jackson's voice was all of a sudden low and hard and flat. So was the look he brought down on me. "It's my thing. Stay out of it."

"You don't know," I barely whispered.

"Yes, I do."

I stopped talking completely, because in Jackson's eyes, I saw that he did know. He knew everything.

Dad was standing with his hand high up on the door, looking down at the floor. If he'd heard any of that, I couldn't tell. He turned to us and smeared his hand all over his face.

"All right," he said. "I'm not blaming either one of you. I'll get this taken care of, and we'll move on. Now both of you, back to bed. You can get a little more sleep before you have to get up for school."

Sleep? He expected us to *sleep*? I crawled under my covers, but I couldn't even close my eyes. Every time I tried, I saw those ugly red letters blotting out our name. The van was the only car we had, and Dad drove it all over Grass Valley like an advertisement to get more work. Who was going to hire him now?

The worse question was: why didn't I talk to Lydia sooner? Why did I think I could do this alone?

It was totally light out when I heard Dad on the phone.

"I'll be there late . . . got some graffiti on my van . . . yeah, I do have to get it taken care of first . . . Look, I'll be there as soon as I can . . . Yes, I'm going to meet your deadline."

Dad's voice got lower and tighter the more he talked. I folded my pillow around my ears, but I could still hear something in my head: Lydia asking him if he'd ever worked for a difficult boss, and Dad saying he had one right now.

He could get fired for this.

My stomach hurt so bad, I could hardly breathe.

But I went to school that day and the next, and I tried to block everything out except working with Colin and waiting to see Lydia on Thursday. Maybe people were whispering about me and my dad, but I didn't hear. I just kept my head down.

Which was why I almost ran into Mrs. Yeats, the principal, in the front hall Wednesday morning before school. She had to put both hands on my shoulders to keep me from stepping on the toes of her sturdy brown shoes.

"Ginger," she said.

"Sorry," I said.

"No need to be. You looked like you were lost in thought." Her chins jiggled a little. "Anything I can help with?"

I shook my head. I had already thought about doing a *Report Alert* on Dad's van, but I knew Kylie was right for once, back when she said whatever happened off the school grounds wasn't the school's business. Besides, I didn't want Mrs. Yeats knowing what they wrote about my dad. Once stuff was in someone's head, it was hard to get it out. Even for a grown-up.

"You really seem to have something on your mind," Mrs. Yeats said. "You're not being bullied like you were before, are you?"

"No," I said. That was the truth. This was not like before. Nothing was.

Mrs. Yeats nodded, her helmet of graying hair not moving. "You'll come see me if I can do anything for you."

"Yes, ma'am," I said.

She smiled. "I like those nice manners."

Yeah, that was me, I thought as I hurried toward the gym. A treasure of integrity with nice manners . . . and a broken-in-half heart.

At least the next day I could see Lydia. Dad was going to be late getting home Wednesday night because his van was being repainted, and Jackson was holed up in his room like the creature Gollum. He'd been like that since Tuesday, except for going to school, which he did wearing black jeans, a black hooded sweatshirt, and a squinty expression. I had my homework done, and I could hardly stand to be alone with myself, so I decided to e-mail Lydia and maybe get started on what I wanted to tell her.

When I got to my inbox, I already had an e-mail from her and my whole body sagged as I read it.

My dear Ginger,

I'm so sorry, but I won't be able to meet with you this Thursday or next. I have doctors' appointments, follow-ups from my surgery. I tried to get them at another time, but they didn't have any other openings. Since we didn't get to talk much Monday either, I feel bad about this, and I hope you'll understand.

But you don't have to stop making good progress like you're doing. I would love for you to start a new list: Things I Like About Me. I know you're going to say that sounds conceited, but it isn't. It's important to know your good qualities, especially right now. That's the start of Step Three, finding a place for yourself so you're better able to handle others not having a place for you. Show someone one of those qualities on your list and see what happens.

In the meantime, don't stop trying.

Blessings,

Lydia

P.S. *Eat healthy food.*

I slid down in the chair and leaned my head over the back of it to look at the ceiling. Small cracks spread out from the overhead light. I thought that's what I must look like inside. Every time I thought I saw some hope, it was just another place splitting open.

Don't stop trying, Lydia wrote. I wasn't sure I could anymore. If she were right there in my kitchen, she would make me food and do some kind of exercise with me that seemed like it didn't make any sense and then it would and I'd be better. She *wasn't* there, though.

But don't stop trying.

I sat up, curled my hand around the mouse, and clicked *reply*.

Dear Lydia.
No.

Dearest Lydia,

Thank you for letting me know you can't be there tomorrow or next week, and I totally understand.

I promise I won't stop trying even though it doesn't seem to be helping much right now. I'll talk to you about that Monday.

I will start the new list. It will be a short one because I don't like that

*much about myself. But what you tell me to do always helps ME. It doesn't
stop other people from doing what they do, but, yeah, it helps me be better.*

Thank you.

Sincerely,

Ginger

I read it three times. Once to make sure I didn't spell anything
wrong and look stupid. The second time to see if I really wanted to
be so honest about it all. And the third time to let what I said sink
into me.

I didn't know it before I wrote it, but it was true. Trying helped
me be better. And I wanted to be better than the girl who blurted
things out to the wrong people and then didn't stand up to them. I
had to be better because it wasn't just about me anymore.

I clicked *send*. And then I went to my room and started that
new list.

After I wrote three things: *I write fantasy in my head, I'm smarter
than people think, I love* The Lord of the Rings, it started to sound
familiar. Because it was. They were all on my list of *Things Nobody
Knows About Me.*

Really?

I pulled out my binder from between the mattresses and looked
at my *Nobody Knows* list. There was also *I love costumes even though I
don't have any.*

That could go on the other list too. I liked that I loved costumes,
even though mine were gone. When my mom first died, I took some
of her scarves and hats and necklaces and her bright green skirt
that swirled, and I kept them in her purple suitcase in the back of
my closet. I used to take them out and put them on and pretend I was
a princess or a damsel in (great) distress, and later the skirt turned
into a cape given to me by the Elves for my journey to Mordor.

The hats were the best, though. They covered up my funky hair and let me be in any time period I wanted. Any time period but the awful one I was in.

But when we moved from Stockton to Fresno, Dad said we had to downsize. He never asked about the purple suitcase before, but that time he opened it and his face got so white his freckles stuck out, and he said I shouldn't keep them, I should move on. That was one of the worst time periods of all.

I shook that off now before the tears could start and considered the look-alike lists again. Show someone one of those qualities, Lydia said. Even if I'd had costumes, I wouldn't have paraded around in them at school. And I sure wasn't going to announce that I had a whole six-volume fantasy story in my head.

I sighed as I slid the binder back into its hiding place. It was so hard to do this without Lydia. But I had to keep trying. I wasn't sure why. I just had to.

The next day, Thursday, I sat down at the lunch table with Colin.

"You're here," he said, face all blushy.

"My meeting got canceled."

He tossed the silky bangs out of his eye. "You want some of my lunch?"

"I brought mine," I said and dumped the contents of my brown bag on the table. "Do you think this looks healthy?"

The place between his eyebrows pinched, just above his glasses, as he checked out my banana and my granola bar and my pickle wrapped in cellophane. That was everything I could find in my kitchen that I thought might be good for me.

"I think so," Colin said. "Maybe you should get some milk too."

I blotched. "I don't exactly have any money."

"I have money."

"No—"

"I'll go get you a milk."

He was gone before I could stop him, and that was probably a good thing because we both probably looked like embarrassed lobsters. I was peeling the wrapper from my granola bar when Riannon slipped into Colin's chair.

Run! my mind screamed at me.

But another voice said, *No, don't stop trying.*

Okay, then. I wouldn't.

"I'm sorry," I said, totally without snarkiness, "but that seat's already taken."

"I know." Riannon's green eyes came together so close they almost crossed. "That's why I'm here. Kylie said to tell you that you aren't very smart."

"She's already told me that herself," I said. My Stone Face was firmly in place.

"She warned you, but you're still friends with Tori so . . ."

So you painted a lie on my dad's van. That made *so* much sense. I pulled my notebook out of my backpack and opened it.

"Are you even listening to me?" Riannon said.

"Yes," I said as I calmly wrote.

"Unless you get it, things could get worse."

I looked up from the notebook. Her *Pointy* Face was firmly in place.

"The Code says not to threaten people," I said. "You did sign it."

"Only so I wouldn't have to go to that stupid class." She rubbed her hand in the air like she was erasing that. "I'm just giving you the facts. Tori isn't in charge. Kylie is. She just says to tell you that until everything gets back to normal, things could get worse."

I wrote, *I'm not sure how they could. You've already messed up just about everything for me.* Then I looked at it. Should I say it? Not all weepy and whiney, but just to show her they couldn't do anything more to hurt me? That I was going to focus on being better now?

Riannon pointed a pink-sparkled nail at the notebook. "Why are you writing down what I'm saying?"

"I'm not writing down what you're saying. I'm writing down what I want to say."

"Well, that's weird. Why don't you just say it?"

"Excuse me," Colin said. "That's my seat."

"I'll sit wherever I want," Riannon said, but she got up and went back to Kylie's table. I guessed. I didn't watch her go.

"Looks like that went well," Colin said, putting the carton and a straw in front of me.

"It kind of did," I said. "Like, for the first time ever." My face felt like it was coming out of a dark place.

"What?" Colin said. "You have an idea, don't you?"

"I think I do. For how our story can end. I don't have all of it but—"

Colin hunched in and so did I. "Let's wait 'til next period to talk about it. Not here."

"Right," I said.

By then lunchtime was almost over, and we had to hurry up and eat while we talked about why Mr. Devon wore a ponytail and whether we would actually want to be Hobbits since they had those hairy feet. We were both smiling without turning tomato-colored when yet another of Those Girls stopped at our table. This time it was Heidi, wrinkling her little pug nose.

"I just have one question," she said.

We both just looked at her.

"Are you two going out or what?"

No, she did *not* just ask that.

"Going out where?" Colin said.

His face was perfectly serious. I stopped shredding the straw wrapper and watched him.

"Out," Heidi said, rolling her eyes so far back I thought she might never find them again. "You know, together."

Colin looked at me. His mouth was still straight, but I could see a gleam behind his glasses. "Have we ever been out anyplace together, Frodo?"

I loved it so much. "No, Sam, we haven't."

"You have pet names for each other," Heidi said. "So you *are* boy-friend and girlfriend."

"Am I your friend?" Colin said to me.

"Of course," I said.

"And I'm a boy, so . . ." He stretched his neck up like he'd just made a great discovery. "Then I'm her boy friend."

"And I'm his girl friend," I said.

"Cute," Heidi said. "You know what I mean."

Colin looked at me again. He was so close to laughing it was practically coming out his ears. "Do you know what she means?"

"Not a clue," I said.

Right then Heidi's picture should have been next to the word *exasperated* in the dictionary.

"What am I supposed to tell Kylie?" she said. She was almost sputtering.

"Well," I said, "like I told Kylie already, I'm mistress of my own tongue, not yours."

I shrugged. The bell rang. Kids scattered like ants, and Heidi scurried off, and Colin finally grinned at me, the whole way.

"You did good," he said.

"So did you," I said.

We were both in a—can I just say *joyous*?—mood when we got to the library. It only took us about fifteen minutes to get our story almost outlined. We had the big Bleakest Moment, and we knew how we wanted it to end. We just didn't know how we were going to get there.

"No worries," Mr. Devon said. "I'll want to see what you have on Monday, and perhaps I can help you along, yes?"

"We can probably figure it out tomorrow," I said.

"Not here," Mr. Devon said. "No school tomorrow. It's Good Friday."

When he went to the counter to check some people out, Colin looked all shy again.

"We could still work together tomorrow," he said. "Just not here."

A giggle came out of me.

"What?" he said.

"Then we would be out somewhere together. Kylie would *love* that."

"Do you care?" Colin said.

I gave that a thought. "No," I said, "actually, I don't. I'll ask my dad if you can come over. My brother will be there—well, you won't see him, but he'll be there, so it should be okay. If it's okay with you, I mean. You don't have to—I just thought maybe . . ."

"What time?" Colin said.

He gave me a big ol' smile, and for a minute, it was better.

Chapter Thirteen

Dad said it was okay for Colin to come, and when I called him, which was way weird because I had never called a boy before, he said he could be there after lunch.

Jackson was in his room, and Dad went to work, so I spent the whole morning cleaning the house and putting wildflowers in a jar on the table and trying to do a snack platter like Lydia always did. That part didn't turn out as well because all we had were cheese crackers in packages, which I unwrapped and arranged on a plate, and iced tea in a big jug.

Then I wondered if Colin would think that was all lame. Of course, the minute he walked in the front door and smiled and handed me a whole jar of pickles, I knew it was going to be okay.

And it *so* was. We spread all our index cards, including the new ones we made the day before, out on the table and organized them into our story about two unlikely heroes named Samantha and Frank who had to defend the Sacred Code by getting past the people who tried to stand in their way, without slaying them, and undergo worse and worse trials until they could return the silver circlets of friendship to the Heights. As they went, the circlets became thinner and thinner, and at the Bleakest Moment, they thought they would dissolve completely before they could reach the Heights and find whatever the Mentors had told them would be revealed to them before the Mentors—the Dwarf and the Gray Wise One—were taken away to deal with the Others who wandered in the Fog of Friendship Confusion.

We had that all in place, and Colin knew which clip art to print on his computer at home to paste on the cards. It was going to be "visually splendid," he said (which he must have picked up from Mr. Devon). We still didn't have our ending: how Samantha and Frank were going to reach the Heights with the circlets weak but intact, and what was going to be revealed to them.

So I got out the snack tray, with some of Colin's pickles on it, and the iced tea, and we sat outside by the grill on the back steps and brainstormed some more. Daffodils had cropped up in random places all over the yard, and the purple and white wildflowers I hadn't picked nodded their heads at the breeze. I think it was what you called *idyllic*.

"Okay," Colin said, "all this time they've been fighting might with right."

"And they're climbing higher," I said, "but the Others aren't giving up, and it's like nobody else is getting it."

"But they don't give up."

"They don't stop trying." I swallowed. If I cried, it would ruin this whole awesome day. Colin might be my friend, but he was still a boy, and since boys didn't cry that much, he probably wouldn't know what to do about tears. Except go home.

"What do you want to do?" Colin said.

"Make this a great ending," I said.

"No." He swirled the ice around in his cup. "I mean in real life. What do you want to do about the people that are spreading rumors about your dad and keeping you from hanging out with your friends and making you feel like a loser?"

I had to close my mouth with my hand.

"I only know because the same thing's going on with me," Colin said. "It's kind of different with guys, but not that much. I used to have a lot of friends in fifth grade, and then we got to sixth and I was getting As and they weren't—because they didn't do their homework, so, duh. And I played basketball because I'm tall for sixth grade and they're shorter. And teachers were okay with me because I was, like, halfway polite and they were acting like jerks. So . . ." Colin shrugged. "They didn't dump me. I would've been kind of okay with that because I really didn't want to hang out with them anymore. They started doing all this stuff to me. Giving me wedgies in P.E."

I didn't know what that was, but it sounded bad, so I just nodded.

"Poking me with pencils in class. Stepping on my homework on the bus. The guy that used to be my best friend?"

"Yeah?"

"He peed on my math book."

"Oh."

Colin's face went way red. "I shouldn't have told you that part."

"It's okay," I said. "Once, Those Girls put all my notes for our science presentation in the toilet and then . . . did the same thing."

"Gross," Colin said. "Worse than that though? The names they called me. Still call me. It's like they're stabbing me in the stomach. My mom tells me to be tough, so I don't even talk to her about it anymore. She thinks it's fine now, but they still tell me I'm a brainer and

I must be a girl because I collect *Lord of the Rings* stuff." He gave me a look with no expression. "I don't know how that makes me a girl."

"I don't either," I said. "I collect, too, but I don't do it because I'm a girl. I do it because I'm me."

We were quiet for a minute. At least on the outside. My mind was talking to me, low and slow and clear. That was it. Samantha and Frank were going to find *themselves* in the Heights, and that would be a place the Others couldn't get to until they left their false selves behind. Like shedding.

"We need cloaks," I said.

"So Samantha and Frank can hide in them," Colin said. "Until they realize they don't have to hide anymore."

"Then you're thinking what I'm thinking?" I said.

"What are you thinking?"

I told him.

"That's what I'm thinking," he said.

"So, can I get this straight?" I said. "Bad stuff is going to happen to them all the way up, but they keep going because they can't change the people who are doing the bad things."

"That's why the heroes don't slay the bad people. The heroes just get stronger."

We looked at each other, and at the same time, we said, "Epic."

We finished our last cards, and Colin left before Dad got home. I was trying to stay in joyous mode, but it was hard for two reasons. One, it was one thing to figure out how the story *should* end, but it wasn't that easy to see how the real-life story *could* end that way.

The other was that it was Friday and Dad was always tired on Friday. He was going to be over Jackson staying in his room and mad because he had to spend money to have his van painted and probably funky because his boss was "difficult." Besides, I felt guilty every time I looked at him. That was one obstacle I couldn't get over.

But when he came in the house, he knocked on my door and poked his head into my room and said, "You want to go shopping?"

"Grocery shopping?" I said. Didn't he already go that week?

"Clothes shopping," he said. "You should have a new dress for Easter."

"Is Goodwill still open this late?" I said.

"Don't know. Thought we'd go to Target."

And get something new?

"Leaving in twenty," he said.

That gave me plenty of time to get my mouth closed.

Target was bustling with moms with carts full of Easter baskets, and bags of candy, and kids begging for stuffed bunnies and dads looking like they wished they were someplace else.

My dad didn't look like that. He looked like he took shopping for a dress very seriously. That was no surprise, since he'd never done it before.

"Pick your color first," he said.

"Green," I said.

Dad looked at me. "Okay. That should work."

We found the dress section in the girls' department. There were three green ones, but two of them were, um, not me. One was poofy, like a tutu, which would have made me look like some kind of freaked-out elf, and one was so short I thought it might be a top. For a five-year-old.

The third one, though, it was green on top, and it came down to a point right below where my waist would be, and then it flared out a little bit into a striped skirt. Like a princess who didn't think she was all that.

"Try that one," Dad said. "But I want to see it on you."

I hesitated.

"What's wrong?"

"I'm not sure it's the right size."

Dad took it and held it up to me. "It should work."

I didn't remind him that I wasn't a plank he was fitting into a floor. I just went to the fitting room and got a plastic number *1* from the lady and went behind a curtain. I kind of jumped when I saw me on all three sides. They didn't put the mirrors inside the dressing rooms at Goodwill.

I tried not to look at myself as I took my other clothes off and slipped into the dress. It was a struggle getting my arms behind me to zip it up, but I felt kind of weird about going out and asking Dad to do it. I peeked out of the curtain, and a lady just going into the cubicle across from mine smiled at me.

"Excuse me?" I said.

"Yes?" she said.

I hesitated a second, but she had nice brown eyes with grand-mother lines around them.

"Would you please zip me up so I can go show this dress to my dad?"

"Absolutely I can!" She hung up her purse and motioned for me to turn around.

I held my breath. It probably wouldn't fit on my smushy body. If it didn't zip up, I wasn't even going to look in the mirror. That way it wouldn't feel so bad when I didn't get it.

"I think this dress was made just for you," the lady said.

"Am I in it?" I asked.

She laughed. "Yes, you're in it."

"It zipped up and everything?"

"And everything. Look at yourself."

She pushed back my curtain, and I stared at myself in the mirrors. It did fit. And nothing squishy bulged out anywhere.

"Your daddy is going to think you're beautiful," she whispered. "But I wouldn't go out in the tennis shoes and socks. What size shoe do you wear? I'll slip out and get you a nice pair of ballet flats."

"Six," I said, "but—"

She was already gone. I turned back to the mirror. This was the nicest thing I ever had on since I outgrew the last outfit Mom bought me before the accident. But this dress was probably way expensive, and I didn't know why Dad even brought me here.

The tag hung from my armpit, so I had to read it in the mirror and figure it out backward. $19.95. That seemed like a lot to me.

The lady came back with some tan slippers that matched the stripes in the skirt and had perfect tiny bows on them. "Slip into these," she said. "I put some little footie things in there."

I put everything on and stood up.

"You're a lovely young lady," she said.

Maybe she needed glasses. But maybe I should just thank her and be happy somebody was being nice to me. Somebody who didn't even have to be.

So I said thank you and held my breath and stepped out of the fitting rooms. Dad had his back to me. He was looking at a display of headbands.

"Um, you want to see?" I said.

He turned around, and things kind of went into slow motion. His hands slid from his hips to his sides, and his rusty eyebrows lifted and pushed his freckles out of the way, and his mouth formed a little *O* that air blew softly out of. It all happened as I watched, and everything else stood still.

"You look like your mom," he said. "Just like her."

"I'm okay, then?"

He nodded.

"It costs $19.95," I said.

"I know."

"I don't have to have the shoes too."

"Yes, you do. And one of these. You like this?"

He picked up a green headband that matched exactly.

"I like it," I said.

Was this really happening?

"All right, get changed," he said. "We'll take it home."

When we got to the check-out, the nice brown-eyed lady was right in front of us.

"I see he approved," she whispered to me.

"He did," I said. "Shoes and everything."

"You look like a young lady who deserves it," she said.

She left, and Dad piled my new outfit onto the counter.

"I didn't know their clothes were this che . . . inexpensive," Dad said. "'Course, I didn't know you liked clothes either." He pulled out his wallet. "You never said."

Maybe because I didn't know that myself?

Maybe I didn't know a lot of things about me, but one thing I did know: I wanted Dad to stay where he was—out in the light.

We had a big storm Saturday night that blew a bunch of branches down from the evergreens and slapped the windows with needles. I was glad it stopped before church, because of my dress and all. I even thanked God for all of it during the sermon. I also looked around for Colin, but he wasn't there. He might not have recognized me anyway.

On the way home, Dad said he wanted to swing by his project and make sure it wasn't damaged in the storm. Jackson didn't care. He was in the behind-seat wearing sunglasses and a black hoodie over the white dress-up shirt Dad made him wear. That meant I got to sit in the front seat, and as soon as we pulled up to the house, I was glad I was getting the windshield view.

The place was, like, out of *Anne of Green Gables*, at least the way I imagined it. There was a wrap-around front porch and two little towers with pointy roofs and white lacy-looking wood around the windows and doors.

"Is this a mansion?" I said as Dad was climbing out of the driver's seat.

"This is a mansion," he said. "Stay put. I won't be long."

He closed the door, and I started dreaming. What was it like to live in this mansion back when it was first built? I bet the girls wore white silk stockings and big bows and slid down the bannisters and read books in the trees. I was imagining breakfasts with whipped cream and strawberries at a long, polished table when a car pulled into the circular driveway.

All dreams dissolved.

The car was small and silver, and it had that circle emblem on the trunk, with the other circle inside it. I could see all the letters this time: *BMW.*

Don't freak, I told myself, even as my breathing got faster. *A lot of people must have cars like that.*

A lot of people like Kylie Steppe, who got out of the passenger seat and stood with her back to me, fluffing out her hair and pulling down the ankles of her pink-and-white-stripped leggings and taking the bags the driver handed to her over the roof of the car.

What was *Kylie* doing here? Did she know these people? Of course she would know them. She was rich too.

One thing was for sure—I didn't want her to see me. I might be halfway to the Heights, but I just didn't want to deal with her today.

I slid slowly down in the seat, and as I went, I saw the driver join Kylie. She was a teenager, taller than Kylie but just as skinny and with the same flippy hair, only longer. They went to the front door, but they didn't knock. Kylie just opened it and went on in.

She *lived* there?

My dad was working for *her* dad?

Before I could slide down any farther in the seat, someone with a shrill voice like the Zabriskis' whistles said something from inside the house. The teenage girl said, in a voice almost like it, "I don't *know*," and whipped her hair around to look over her shoulder.

I froze, and so did she. At first I thought she saw me, but then I realized she was staring at the side of our van. Even from the street, I could see her eyes go round and scared.

"Move, Kylie!" she said, and she flung herself inside the house and crashed the door shut behind her.

"Don't slam it!" the first whistle voice said. "It's brand-new!"

I sat there and shook. I looked back at Jackson, but he was slumped over like he was asleep or pretending to be. It was just me then. And now I knew for sure. I did before, but I could never figure out how Kylie could get to my house in the middle of the night. It was that girl—probably her sister. She looked way guiltier than I ever felt, and I'd felt some pretty serious guilt. Yeah. They did it.

They did it, and I should tell someone. But as I watched my dad walk toward the van, the dad who bought me a beautiful dress and was looking at me differently ever since, I knew it couldn't be him I told. What was he going to do? Go to his boss and say his daughters messed up his van when he needed this big job for us?

"Looks good," he said when he climbed back into his seat. "You feel like burgers for dinner? That could be Easter, right?"

"Sure," I said.

"Picked up some potato salad . . ."

I didn't hear the rest of the menu because I was thinking about the other reason I couldn't tell him or anybody else. I still didn't have any proof. I saw a car like their BMW that night. I just saw Kylie's sister look like the police were coming after her with handcuffs. Kylie was Twittering or whatever about Dad all over the place. But that was all. I still had nothing.

So Monday during lunch, I didn't tell Lydia anything after all. And when she asked me if I had a nice Easter, I didn't write it down, I didn't think it through, I just blurted out, "Every time I think things are getting better, something else bad happens. Yesterday was all about Jesus saving us, but how come He doesn't care about *me?* Why do we have to do this all on our own—people like Colin and me—why?"

Lydia slid a quesadilla toward me across the little table, but I ignored it.

"You're not doing it on your own," she said. "God's there."

"Choosing to make it hard so I'll get character?"

Lydia pulled in her chin. "Say again?"

"God *chooses* for bad stuff to happen to people so we'll get stronger. I don't want to be stronger. I just want to be happy for more than five minutes."

I opened my eyes wide so my face wouldn't crumple. Lydia shook her head at me.

"Who *ever* told you that?" she said.

"A preacher. In a sermon."

"When?"

"Back when we lived in—I don't even remember." My throat got thick. "Could we not talk about this?"

"This is one time when I'm going to insist we talk." Lydia scooted to the very edge of her chair. "I hope that preacher didn't actually say that. I hope you just misunderstood. Ginger, that is *not* what God does. Would *your* father leave you out in the woods someplace and tell you to try to survive so you would be stronger?"

"No."

"Then why on *earth* would your heavenly Father, who loves you more than anyone else, possibly *make* bad things happen to you so you'll be wise and strong?"

"I don't know," I said. I'd stopped trying not to cry.

"I don't either. Nobody really knows why bad, hard things happen to us. Sometimes it's because *we* make bad choices. But God forgives us and helps us through. Sometimes it's because other people make bad choices. God forgives them and helps us through. Sometimes it doesn't make any sense at all. God comforts us and, again, helps us through." She squeezed her little hands together. "I don't mean to preach at you, Ginger, but somebody has to replace that other sermon. We do learn and get stronger through the hard stuff, but that's because God is love, not because God's putting us through some kind of obstacle course."

"He's not like Coach," I said.

"Oh, *heavens* no!"

I still shook my head.

"What part of that doesn't make sense to you?" Lydia said.

"What if I don't pray that much—because I'm mad at God? I bet God doesn't help then."

"You're mad at God for taking your mom."

"Yes."

"That shows you believe in God. You wouldn't be mad at someone who you didn't think existed. Besides . . ." She tilted her head of big curls at me in that wonderful way she had. "You have other people praying *for* you."

"You," I said.

"And not just me. Your Tribelet."

"Even now? I thought they would hate me for ditching them. Only, I had to protect my dad and my brother *and* Tori. Kylie hates it that Tori has more friends than her now and people actually respect Tori, and she can't stand it, so she used me to get at Tori, and everything got all messed up and it ended up not helping anybody."

"Exactly," Lydia said. "Exactly." She cleared her throat. "There's something else I wanted to talk to you about."

Her voice changed. My stomach warned me with a sharp pain.

Lydia pulled two sheets of paper out of her red bag and handed me one. "Did you send this to me?"

It was a typed message with my e-mail address at the top.

Dearest Lydia, it said.

Gee, thanks for letting me know you don't care enough about me to change your stupid doctors' appointments to meet with me like you promised you would.

I decided to stop trying anyway. It doesn't seem to be helping much right now. So I won't be talking to you on Monday or ever.

And I'm not going to start that lame list. I don't like myself. Actually I hate myself, and you won't even help me with that because you're not going to show up. I can't stop other people from doing what they do because I deserve it anyway.

Thanks for nothing.

Insincerely,

My hands were shaking so hard I couldn't even read my name. "I didn't write this," I said. "I swear I didn't."

"You don't have to swear to it. I believe you."

Lydia's face was perfectly calm. I knew mine wasn't.

She handed me the other sheet of paper. "How about this one?"

"Is it like that one?" I said.

"Just read a few lines and tell me if you sent it."

I looked down at the paper, sure the words were going to come up and strangle me like a boa constrictor.

Dear Tori,

This is the stupidest poem ever, and I've read a lot of poems, so I should know.

1. *You tried to make it like a real sonnet, and it's not even close.*
2. *It's supposed to be about your best quality, but you don't have one so I don't know why you even tried.*

I couldn't read the rest.

"I didn't write this either," I said. "Does Tori think I did? Is that why she said I was mean about her poem?"

"She was stunned at first, yes, but after we talked about it, she thought maybe Kylie made you do it." Lydia folded her neat hands. "I just couldn't see that, but I couldn't tell her what you and I have been talking about because it's confidential."

I looked at the tops of the papers, both with my e-mail address at the top. "I don't get it," I said. "How can these look like they came from me when they didn't?"

"Somebody got into your e-mail account," Lydia said. "Have you ever given anyone your password?"

"No," I said. "Not even my brother. It's written down in a book my dad keeps at home, but nobody ever comes to my house."

"Do you use your e-mail account here at school?"

"Sometimes. Maybe once or twice."

"Was anybody around, close enough to see you type in your password?"

"No. Nobody ever gets that close."

The bell rang, and I started to spiral down into a little hole.

Lydia tapped her hand on the arm of her chair. "No, no, there will be none of that. You're starting to figure this out, and you can't stop now. You have to keep trying." She nodded, hard. "I will try to get to the bottom of this e-mail thing, and in the meantime, we'll keep praying. Agreed?"

"Okay," I said.

"Do you feel safe?"

My turn to nod. "It's all coming out now. They can't do anything else to me."

Lydia twitched her eyebrows. "Well, just in case, *Report Alert* is still the rule."

"Yes, ma'am," I said.

Keep trying. That's what I told myself as I got ready for fifth period. Those Girls had ways of bullying that I didn't even know were possible, ways I didn't understand. But I was going to keep trying.

Besides, Colin and I had our storyboard to present to Mr. Devon.

He did a lot of "mmming" and "aahing" and nodding as we talked and showed him our pictures, and when we got to the Bleakest Moment he stopped us and said, "Do you see what you've accomplished here? It's just as Tolkien does it." His ponytail swung as he leaned over the table. "The closer Samantha and Frank get to the Heights, the stronger they are, and the harder the Others work to hold them back until they can't stop them because they have no power against True Selves."

I straightened way up. "Could I ask you something?" I said.

"Of course."

"Do you think that's what happens in real life?"

"I *know* that's what happens in real life," Mr. Devon said. "I've had to get past many, many Others in my life, so I know whereof I speak. This, my young friends"—he smiled down at our storyboard—"This is brilliant. The fair would be a wasteland without it."

"You mean, we get a booth?" Colin said.

"You have a better opportunity than that," Mr. Devon said. "You have one of the slots to do a presentation to all the fifth-graders, and of course our sixth-graders, the hosts. Eight minutes can hardly do it justice, but I think we can work with that, don't you?"

I was still back on "presentation."

"Do you mean, like, act it out or something?" I said.

"Whatever you decide would be most effective." Mr. Devon rubbed his hands together like he always did when he thought something was about to be even more brilliant than it already was. "The fair is Tuesday. That gives you a little over a week to prepare."

"We'll be ready," Colin said. When Mr. Devon left us, he said to me, "Right?"

I was *still* on the word *presentation*. To the whole fifth grade and our sixth grade. Those Girls. The BBAs.

The Tribelet.

"Right," I said.

Then we looked at each other and I said, "Can you come over?" at the same time he said, "Can I come over?" We finished with, "Saturday?"

We had until then to figure out what we were going to do, which we worked on at lunch and during fifth period and sometimes even before school for a few minutes if we had time.

In the meantime, that tension that was building before? It kept climbing.

Chapter Fourteen

T his time it was the teachers who were making people stress out. Well, not all people. Just Kylie and Those Girls.

In Spanish class, Mrs. Bernstein was all over Kylie because she was being so bossy about the Spanish booth.

In science, Mr. V made Those Girls split up and be lab partners with other people, and then he watched them like detectives on TV when they're on a stakeout, only he did it with his big elastic smile on his face.

Kylie got so prickly about it she was even snappy with Heidi and Izzy and Riannon. In math class, I heard her tell them all to stop copying her and get a life. They looked as confused as I was. I mean, if they *didn't* copy her hair and her fingernail polish and her Barbie doll smile, they basically didn't *have* a life. Nobody knew better than me how she could take that away.

If I let her.

The Kylie Stress really hit the wall Thursday in the lunchroom. It was pretty calm in there, for the sixth grade anyway, and Colin and

I were still brainstorming on how we were going to do our presentation, when Mr. Jett marched down the aisle between the tables. His arms pumped and his mustache quivered and his entire bald head was shiny red.

"He's on a mission," Colin whispered to me.

And evidently that mission was about Those Girls because he halted (not stopped, *halted*) at their table and stuck his hands on his hips.

"Danner!" he said, pointing his chin at Heidi.

"*What?*" Heidi said.

Kylie jabbed her so hard I clutched my own side. She put on the Barbie smile.

"Is something wrong, Mr. Jett?" she said.

"I wasn't talking to you, Steppe. I was talking to Danner."

Once again with the chin jab. By then the whole cafeteria was silent as a movie theater when you get to the scary part. I could see Heidi's 'tude draining from her face. Any other teacher would take you aside and bust you, but we all knew Mr. Jett was more into taking people down in public.

"I just got a message from Lydia Kiriakos. You know her?"

"The bullying lady?" Heidi said in an almost-whisper.

"The *anti*-bullying lady. She wanted to know when I wanted to reschedule your meeting with her since you got there late the last time I sent you."

Kylie's entire group had *oops* on their faces. Even Kylie's eyes shifted like she was looking for the emergency exit.

"Imagine my surprise," Mr. Jett said, "because I never sent you to her in the first place."

"Heidi kind of sent herself down," Kylie said. "She knew she violated the Code so . . ."

He slammed his palm on the table, and the whole lunchroom jumped. "What is with this group and your lying? Huh? Lunch detention for all of you. With me. Tomorrow."

"Aren't you supposed to send us to that Lydia person?" Kylie said.

"Is she brain damaged or what?" Colin muttered to me.

"I'm supposed to send *you* to Mrs. Yeats, and you know what she would do. So I suggest you stop pushing me."

Yeah, they took that suggestion.

But as Mr. Jett marched back up the aisle and the bee-buzzing began, Kylie shook off the Barbie face and aimed her blue eyes right at Tori.

Like it was *Tori's* fault they lied to try to see what was going on with Lydia and me? Like the Tribelet was to blame for *any* of this? Like . . .

My thoughts tripped over each other and fell in a pile because Kylie tossed her hair and turned to me. I guessed she was looking at me, although her eyes were in such tight slits I wasn't sure she could even see me.

Just in case, I put on my Stone Face and waited for my stomach to hurt.

But it didn't. Somehow, it just didn't.

That was lunchtime. Fifth period, Mr. Devon got interrupted about ten times with people coming in to use the computers. By sixth, there was so much whispering and people sneaking looks at their cell phones, I was getting afraid that they were starting up about my dad again, although I didn't know what worse things they could say. I got a little stressed out myself and got a pass to the restroom from Mrs. Bernstein so I could regroup.

I washed my hands and went over all the cards and my steps and everything in my head. I could do this. No matter what, I could climb to the Heights. I could take off the Stone Face and go for it.

I looked up at the mirror to watch myself morph back into me, but somebody else's reflection was there with mine. It was Shelby, and her lips were in a frightened bunch.

"I just thought you should know," she said, still looking at me in the mirror.

"Okay," I said.

"Kylie's spreading it around that they're backing off of Tori and her friends. She calls them the G-Gs. For Goody-Goodies."

"Okay," I said again. Shelby was getting the words out fast like she needed to just say them and escape. I wasn't going to slow her down.

"But they're planning to take down the anti-bullying campaign at the fair next week and make it look stupid in front of everybody."

I watched my eyes bulge in the mirror. "Does Tori know?"

Shelby nodded. "I told her. But I thought you should know too because you're doing so good and everything. You can't let them take you down either."

I turned and looked at her instead of her reflection. "They can't," I said.

Shelby looked at me through her veil of hair before she left. I reached for a paper towel.

But then I heard the door swish open and I heard her say, "You're way braver than me."

Yeah, well, I didn't feel so brave the next morning in first period P.E., and this time it wasn't about Kylie and Those Girls. It was about having to take the final obstacle course test.

"This is pass/fail, people," Coach announced in his pit bull voice. "You do everything, you pass. You don't, you fail. Simple as that."

I looked over at Tori's team. Ophelia had her arm slung around Winnie, and Tori was giving her a thumbs-up. This was good news for Winnie because she'd gotten to the top of the wall the day before.

It was miserable news for me.

"The two teams that win—boys and girls—get extra credit points."

Kylie poked Riannon, who of course poked Heidi. But Heidi shook her head. By the time Riannon gave Izzy a jab and Izzy said, "Is that even fair?" Coach had already walked away. I knew the whistle blow was coming, so I covered my ears, but not before I heard Riannon say, "We're not getting bonus points with Ginger on our team."

Kylie let her eyes glance over me. "We don't need bonus points."

My stomach wanted to know what *that* meant. But my stomach wasn't in charge. I took a deep breath and followed Coach to the starting line.

It was kind of exciting, actually, with people sprinting and climbing and jumping their best and their teams screaming, "Go! You got this! You can totally do it!"

I even liked doing some of it. Coach made Winnie and me be some of the last ones so we wouldn't slow anybody behind us down. Once Winnie got going, I ran my fastest and wriggled through the tunnel without getting stuck in the middle like I did the first time and jumped all the hurdles without knocking any of them down. The rope was a challenge, but I could hear Mitch yelling, "Look up! Use your legs too!" and I made it up and didn't even have hand burns.

And then came the wall. It loomed over me, and I could almost hear it saying, *Are you serious? You're going to climb ME? Why do you even try?*

Because I never stopped trying.

"Talking to it isn't going to get you up there."

Coach was standing right next to me. I looked at him and looked away fast, but I saw enough to know I'd said it out loud.

"But that's the right attitude," he said. "You gotta try. Let's go."

I did try. I really did. I kept my eyes up, and I reached for the next handhold and found the ones below with my feet. I was halfway up before I realized it.

"You're doing it," Winnie whispered from above me on her side.

I was. I was doing it.

I stretched to the next plaster "rock" with my hand and felt around with my foot. It didn't land anyplace. I didn't know where the hold was because I'd never been up this far. My leg flailed around, but still it didn't find the bump. So I did the worst thing you can do when you're climbing the wall.

I looked down.

Way down, or at least it seemed that way to me. Mitch was yelling, "Look up! Look *up!*" The soccer girls all had their hands over their mouths. Kylie was examining her nail polish.

I closed my eyes and tried to make myself get calm. There was a foothold there someplace. Everybody else found it. Why couldn't I?

Maybe I didn't have to. Maybe I could just get the rest of the way up with my hands.

I let go of my lower hand and groped for the rock just above me. But it was out of my reach and my other hand was shaking and sweating . . . because the only thing holding me now was one slippery palm.

"I'm gonna fall!" I cried out.

"No, you're not, Ginger," Winnie said. She was even with me, on her way down. "Hold on!"

But there was nothing to hold on to. My hand shook off of its rock, and I plunged toward the ground. I'd been right that first day. The mattresses weren't thick enough. All the air came out of me when I hit, and I was sure I felt my brain slosh inside my skull.

"Everybody to the locker rooms!" Coach barked.

I tried to keep my eyes closed as the feet all retreated and left us in quiet, but Mrs. Zabriski told me to look at her.

I did, and they both peered into my eyes.

"You're okay," she said. "Can you sit up?"

I struggled to get myself upright and shook my head. "I'm not okay," I said. "I failed."

"Not yet." Coach's voice was a low growl, but his eyes didn't look mad. "You gave it a shot. You can do a retest on just the wall Monday. I'll let Iann climb it with you, and she can coach you. Fair enough?"

"Okay," I said, although my head was spinning and I knew it wasn't from the fall. *Coach* was saying this?

"I'm doing this because you have a good attitude," he said.

Mrs. Zabriski gave a really loud sniff. "Which is more than I can say for some other people in this class."

"Some other people in this class" didn't say a word to me for the rest of the day, not even to ask if I was okay, which was perfectly fine with me. Except I knew from Shelby that ignoring me and the Tribelet was part of their takedown plan. I kept watching Tori and Winnie and Mitch and Ophelia, but they didn't act worried at all.

By fifth period, I stopped worrying, too, because Colin and I decided how to do our presentation. We couldn't exactly act it all out in eight minutes, but we could read it with the voices, and Mr. Devon took a picture of each card so he could turn them into a PowerPoint presentation that everybody could see while we read.

"This goes beyond epic," Colin said.

He was right. But it was hard Saturday when I was getting ready for him to come over not to picture the fair without seeing the anti-bullying booth being torn down or something. If the Tribelet knew, Lydia knew. They wouldn't just let it happen.

But somehow that didn't seem like enough. So while I was

arranging granola bars and banana slices on a plate, I stopped and made sure nobody was around, and I whispered, "If you do care, God, will you please help us?"

Colin and I rehearsed our reading for, like, two hours, and while we were having snacks at the table, Colin said, "I have a brilliant idea."

"Are you sure it's brilliant?" I said. "Mr. Devon only uses that when something is really, really awesome."

"This is." Colin hunkered over the table a little. "What if we didn't read our parts? What if we did them from memory?"

"Are you kidding? I'm freaked out enough just reading in front of all those hundreds of people. What if I forget my lines?"

Colin's eyebrows all twisted up together in the middle. "You already have the whole thing memorized. You weren't even looking at the script last time we did it. *You're* the one who gave me the idea."

"But that's here in my house, with nobody else watching."

"You need an audience?"

Dad let the screen door bang shut behind him and stood between us and the kitchen. A big blob of sweat covered the front of his T-shirt.

"Can I have some of this iced tea?"

He was *asking* me?

"Yes, sir," I said.

Dad opened the freezer and got out an ice tray. "Why don't you practice your thing on me?"

"That would be awesome," Colin said.

No, that would be a miracle. I didn't say anything as Dad poured tea in his glass and wiped his forehead with the back of his hand.

"Get set up then," Dad said. "I'll be in the living room."

Colin was smiling his whole smile. I was not. Maybe I *could* do the whole presentation from memory in front of every fifth- and sixth-grader in Grass Valley, but I couldn't do it in front of my dad. First of all, he wasn't even acting like my dad and—

"Are you in a trance or something?" Colin said. "Let's prop the board up near him so he can see it, and we'll try it without our scripts. It'll be easier to get into the voices and stuff that way."

All I was into was finding a way not to do this. Dad didn't know characters in stories were real to me. He didn't know I could practically become them. He was going to think this was silly and ridiculous and lame.

But Colin was all jazzed about it. He set the storyboard up on the couch next to Dad and got some chairs from the table, in case we wanted to use them as props to stand on or whatever, he said. The whole while he was doing it, his face was light pink, the way it got sometimes when he was excited about a thing.

Our thing. And my thing too.

Okay. I could try. After all, it wasn't like climbing a wall.

Well, not a real one anyway.

Colin and I got in position, and he started us off. His voice was different from when we just did it for ourselves. It was a little deeper, and it had a lot of expression, like this was super-important stuff and the "audience" should listen carefully. When it was my part of the introduction, I didn't expect any voice to come out of me at all. But when I spoke, mine was different too. Not like a bullhorn or a whine. Dad's chin came up, and his eyes opened wider. So I kept going.

It was fun doing it without paper in my hand. Colin and I both used the chairs to sit, lean, put a foot up on. When we got to the part where Samantha and Frank reached the Heights, we were both standing on them, without even planning it.

On the final lines, we looked at each other and then out at the Others. Well, Dad, who I'd kind of forgotten was still there.

Maybe it was still Dad. The man who sat there on the couch crinkled all his freckles into a smile and clapped his big hands. For a long time.

"So it was okay?" Colin said.

"Don't I look like it was okay? It was great. You kids—this is good."

That was Dad for "brilliant." It had to be because I'd never actually heard those words come out of his mouth before.

"Now you need outfits," he said.

"You mean costumes?" Colin said.

He turned to me, all smiley, but I looked down.

Colin's smile faded by a half. "I have one I could wear, but if you don't, I won't wear one either."

"I don't have any costumes anymore," I told the floor.

"Hold on," Dad said.

He went down the hall, and I stood there feeling blotchy.

"He liked it," Colin said.

"Yeah," I said.

"I wish my mom was as nice as your dad."

My head came up. "I bet your mom is too," I said. "I didn't even know my dad could be this nice, so maybe we just don't see it when we're around them every day."

"My mom would never sit there and watch like he did. She probably won't even take off work to come Tuesday."

"But there has to be *some* nice in her. She takes you to church."

"No, she doesn't. I go by myself. And I couldn't even go on Easter because we went to her boyfriend's for an egg hunt. Like that means anything when she doesn't even care about God."

He had gone from light pink to strawberry. I looked out the window so he could get himself back together. Dad came back down the hall just in time.

"I kept a few things of your mom's," he said.

He was holding a brown tunic thing with a wide belt and a floppy green hat and something green draped over his arm.

"That's perfect!" Colin said.

"You have a cloak or a cape or something?" Dad said to Colin.

"Yeah, it's dark green."

"Good." Dad opened up the green velvety thing and put it around my shoulders. "Guess you'll have to pin it up some so you don't trip over it."

No way. Even I couldn't trip in something so elegant. It spilled down from my shoulders to the ground in one long train of wonderfulness.

"Your mom used to wear that when we'd go out someplace special," Dad said. "And she'd make me wear a tie." He swallowed, like it was hard to do. "You look more like her than ever in that."

"You look like Samantha," Colin said.

Maybe so. Or maybe I just looked like Ginger.

Chapter Fifteen

The only thing that even dared to pinch at my stomach Monday morning was having to do the wall climb test first period. But when I got to the locker room, there was a sign on the door saying no class because of preparation for the fair. We were all supposed to go to the gym to help set up.

But I went straight to Coach, who was in Mrs. Zabriski's office just off the locker room.

"Um, what about my test?" I said.

"We'll have to reschedule," he said.

"So, when? Sir."

"Sir," he said. "Wow."

He sounded a little bit sarcastic, but just a little. Not like he was exactly making fun of me.

"Listen, don't sweat it for now," he said. "Just do your fair thing."

Mrs. Zabriski raised her cropped-hair head from her clipboard. "I heard you're doing a special presentation with . . ." She snapped her fingers like she was searching for his name.

"Colin. Yes, ma'am."

She dropped the clipboard on the desk, and I jumped. What *now*?

"All right, that's it," she said. "Who are you and what have you done with Ginger Hollingberry?"

"I'm sorry?" I said.

"That's a compliment," Mrs. Z said. She waved a wiry hand at me. "Go. Do your thing."

"Yes, ma'am," I said and hurried out.

Behind me, I heard her say, "That is not the same kid."

We spent all of first period helping get the booths set up—they were fold-up walls you could hang stuff on—and Mr. Devon showed Colin and me where we would be standing for our presentation. When Colin told him about the chairs, he borrowed two big wooden cubes, painted black, from the eighth-grade drama teacher. They were way better than my kitchen table chairs. He promised we could practice with them fifth period.

I didn't get to meet with Lydia during lunch because Mrs. Yeats came to the cafeteria while we were eating to drill us on how to be good hosts and hostesses to the fifth-graders the next day. Basically, she told us *to* follow the Code and *not* to burp, belch, or make other disgusting noises. I guessed you didn't get to be principal without knowing about BBAs.

Lydia sent me a message through Mr. Devon that she would be there for tomorrow's presentation, and that made me a whole lot less nervous. After we rehearsed with the big black cubes in the gym, with the PowerPoint going on the screen above and behind us, I wasn't nervous at all. In fact, I couldn't wait for it to be tomorrow.

I actually forgot about the planned takedown by Kylie and Those Girls until I got to sixth period. We were supposed to bring in our stuff for the Spanish booth, and Kylie was perched on the front edge of Mrs. Bernstein's desk, checking everybody off like some big important bird. Until Mrs. B made her get off.

Kids were running to their lockers to get things they forgot and picking up stuff from the shelves to look at them—like maracas and pottery bowls and a jar of what somebody claimed were Mexican jumping beans. It was chaos, but the good kind because people were laughing and checking out each other's stuff and saying, "That is *sweet!*" Well, the girls did. The boys were all trying to figure out how to get the jumping beans open.

And then Kylie stood up on a chair and said, "Could everybody just stop talking! I can't think!"

Tori made a motion like she was zipping her lips closed.

I pressed mine together, just in case.

"Thank you," Kylie said, even though only about half the class had actually stopped talking. "If you haven't checked your assignment in with me, line up here."

"Please," Mrs. Bernstein said. "And, Kylie, get down."

"I was *going* to," Kylie said.

She said something else to Mrs. Bernstein, but I didn't hear it because there was a commotion at the door.

"That is so cool!" Tori said.

Shelby came in with a huge sombrero on her head and a bright blanket thing on her shoulder, which I thought the culture book said was a serape, and a big potted cactus in her arms.

"*Excelente!*" Mrs. Bernstein said. "This is going to *make* the booth!"

Tori started clapping and Mitch whistled, which the BBAs joined in on, and Mrs. Bernstein didn't try to stop it. It might have been the best moment we ever had in Spanish class.

But it obviously wasn't a good moment for Kylie. Especially when

Mrs. Bernstein put the sombrero on Kylie's head and it came down over her eyes. It looked like the hat was wearing her, so who wouldn't laugh?

Kylie yanked it off and plunked it on Mrs. Bernstein's desk and said, "I'm not wearing that in my booth."

"I will!" said Izzy, who had the perfect sized head for it.

"Whatever," Kylie said. I was surprised *her* head didn't just fly right off.

I got in line behind the soccer girls to get my map checked off. I'd drawn Mexico on a piece of white plywood my dad gave me. I colored and labeled it with the mountains and everything, and I'd even glued on small pictures in some places.

"That's really good," Evelyn said. She was standing behind me with a plastic bag. A thing of Doritos peeked out the top. "I only brought food, but you . . . that's, like, professional."

"So are you going to show me your thing or not?" Kylie said. "The bell's about to ring."

I stepped up to her. It was the first time I'd seen her up close since class started, and now I could see tiny beads of perspiration on her upper lip and under her eyes. I didn't think Kylie would ever sweat. Not only that, but her splashy hair was jammed behind her ears and her breath was coming out in fast huffs. She wasn't the poster girl for cool right then.

I turned my board around for her to see. Her eyes got wide, and then she squinted them down, and, yep, the lip curled. Nostrils blocked, the whole thing.

"What is *that*?" she said.

"Kylie," Mrs. Bernstein said. "You are out of con—"

"It's a map of Mexico," I said. I propped it against the desk. "You can go ahead and check me off."

I didn't wait for her to say anything. I just turned and headed back to my desk, weaving among the people who were all having conversations with each other with their eyes. Except Mitch, who said, "Wow."

When I got to my seat, there was a folded piece of paper waiting for me. I looked around to see if anybody was watching, wanting me to open it.

"I think it came from the office," Ophelia said. "I was standing by the door and some eighth-grader brought it."

That should be okay then. I still opened it with only my finger-tips, though. I didn't want the words exploding at me.

But I puffed out a breath of relief. It was from Coach Zabriski. *I'll retest you after school. Dress out and meet me at the climbing wall.*

The bell rang, and my first thought was that I should get a message to Jackson and tell him that I'd be late getting home. But really, how long could it take? And Coach said Mitch would be there . . .

I looked up, but she and just about everybody else were gone. Except Kylie, who was in the corner being talked to by Mrs. Bernstein. They had their own wall of tension to climb.

Okay, I decided as I left the room and headed downstairs. I could do this. If I could do a presentation in front of my dad and not be nervous about doing it for, like, two hundred kids, and if I could give Kylie the Stone Face and not get all hysterical because she acted like she hated my map—if I could do all that, I could climb this wall.

It didn't hit me until I was halfway into my sweats in the locker room. What if I pretended I was Samantha climbing to the Heights? Wouldn't that make it less scary? If she could do it, so could I because, uh, I *was* her.

I finished getting changed and let myself out the back door. It was strange being on the obstacle course by myself. It looked bigger and, as Mr. Devon would say, more formidable without all the other kids and Coach. But I'd done most of it. That helped.

Come to think of it, where *was* Coach?

I wished I'd brought the note out with me so I could check and make sure I was right, that it said today, after school. I was certain of it, though. So I sat on a bench we never got a chance to sit on during class and watched the cars leave the back parking lot. It was also strange to see Mr. V and Mr. Jett and Mrs. Fickus get into their Volkswagens and SUVs. They actually had lives away from us.

Before long, the faculty parking lot was pretty much empty and the school seemed eerie-quiet behind me. I *must* have made a mistake, right? Struggling not to stick the *Stupid* label back on myself, I went to the door to go back into the locker room.

It was locked.

I banged on it, but nobody came.

Okay, double strange. Maybe I should go around to the front of the school and come back to the gym that way.

Yeah, and what if Coach came out while I was inside and thought I'd dissed him and I'd fail the retest without even taking it?

Something rumbled. It took me a minute to realize it was faraway thunder. The sky was darker than it usually was at this time of day. Which was, what? Four o'clock by now? Maybe later? It was hard to tell with charcoal-colored clouds blocking out the light. Yeah, I probably should take a chance and go around to the front of the school and see if there was anybody still here.

Just as I got up from the bench, the back door opened and a guy stuck his head out. I didn't know him. He looked like a teenager, maybe older because he had one of those almost beards that looked like dirt on his chin, and his face was harder than a middle school kid's had a chance to get.

"You Ginger?" he said, hardly opening his mouth.

"Uh-huh."

"So, you're supposed to do a practice run and Coach'll be right out."

"But—"

"That's all I know."

"Wait!"

But the door shut and I was still standing there in the storm-gathering dark.

A practice run? Alone? With no spotters and—I looked over at the wall—no mats?

I walked slowly toward it, thoughts spinning. He said Coach would be right out. Maybe a practice run meant "assess" the climb like he was always telling us to do.

I had never actually done that. I'd never stood there and figured out where the handholds and footholds were before I tried to go up the wall. All I could ever think about was how terrified I was and how if I ever did get to the top I would probably wet my pants.

All right then. I got to the bottom of the wall and took in a deep breath and looked up. At first, it was just a bunch of fake plaster rocks sticking out all random. But if I could just remember where they all were . . .

I almost bopped my own self in the head. Of course I could remember. If I could memorize a whole eight-minute script, and if I could quote Tori's sonnet right there on the spot, and if I could close my eyes and see the nasty notes and threatening letters Those Girls had dropped on me, then I could totally remember where all the handholds and the foot places were. All I had to do was study it and then get into Samantha mode.

I got it all like a picture in my mind. Then I imagined I was wearing the cloak I would take off when I got to the top because there would be no need to hide myself anymore. Finally, I let the vision take place of Frank, well, Colin, climbing below me, and both of us having a thin, disappearing circlet on our arms, ready to save true friendship from those who would take it down.

My mind was ready. I looked up and reached for the first hand-hold. I saw the next one in my head, and I found it. My feet followed. The next one and the next one—in my mind and in my hands and in my feet. Another and another. Climbing. Just like going up a ladder. One more—hands, feet, and I was there. I was at the top. I had hit the Heights.

"I did it!" I cried out to no one. "I made it!"

There was only one problem. I'd never gotten that high before . . . and I didn't know how to get down.

"Okay," I said to myself this time. "I can do this. It's the same going the other way, only backward. Right? I mean, right?"

I had to study it again. I had to look.

I did it again. I made the worst mistake. The ground was faraway and spinning. I was more terrified than I had ever been.

I forced myself to look up, but there was nothing to see but the tops of the evergreens, disappearing into the too-soon dark of the coming storm. But I squirmed higher until I could hang onto the very top of the wall. And then I clung there, like a baby koala.

Call for help. Yeah. Do that.

I took a deep breath and turned my head back toward the school. I couldn't see the whole front, but I could see all of the back, and there was only one car left in the lot, a pickup truck with ladders sticking out of it. The janitor was still here.

"Help me!" I shouted.

But the wind picked up my voice and carried it away from the building. I tried again and then again, over and over until nothing came out but a croak. As the sky got darker and the wind blew harder, I even tried calling out to cars passing on the street behind the school. Nobody even slowed down. If I ever got down from here, I was always going to look up when I was riding with Dad—just in case stranded kids were stuck up on walls and needed help.

Except, who else would be clueless enough to get themselves into this situation—again?

Dad would be home by now, and he was going to be mad and all the niceness of buying me a new dress and watching my presentation and giving me costumes was going to go away. Especially since I didn't tell Jackson I was staying after school. Why didn't I?

I pressed my face into the plaster on the top of the wall. Okay, I *had* to get down. I couldn't stop trying, right? Pretty soon it was going to start raining and the thunder was going to get closer. I needed to get to the bottom before that happened.

I pawed at the plaster below with one foot and found something. I let my foot rest on it, but it slipped and I barely grabbed the top of the wall again before I fell. I'd fallen before, but not from this high. And there were mats there then. Not thick enough, but I would have traded anything for them now.

"What am I going to do?" I said. "God, what am I going to do?"

God. Lydia said God didn't choose to give us hard things to handle. I'd done a fine job of that on my own. But she said God would help. She said she prayed for me and the Tribelet did. She said it might not change what was happening, but God would help me handle it.

"Then please do," I whispered. "Please help me now."

"Please, please, please," I said as I held on tight with my hands and searched for a place with my other foot. I connected with something this time and it held. Now another one, and then I could move my hands again. Backwards from the way I went up.

It helped to whisper, so I kept on. "Please, please . . . don't stop trying . . . next foot . . . there it is . . . please, please . . ."

Something wet hit the top of my head, and another drop splashed on my hand and I felt it run down my arm. How much farther could I have to go? It felt like I'd been climbing down forever.

"Don't look down," I whispered. "Just keep going, please, please . . ."

A loud whoop shattered the air and blue light flashed over me . . . and over me . . . and over me. I jerked and felt myself start to fall. I cried out, "No!" but my fingers slid away from the wall.

All my breath left me and pain took its place, knocking into my back and my head as I slammed into the ground. I gasped, but no air came in. All I wanted to do was get up and run, but I couldn't.

"Don't move," a man's voice said. "Just be still."

"We need an ambulance," a woman said.

I tried to tell them no.

"Just stay calm, sweetie," the woman said.

"Please!"

That was me talking.

"We're the police," the woman said. "We're here to help you."

"No," I said. "I want my dad."

And then I started to cry.

Chapter Sixteen

M y memory was good for some things, but I couldn't remember much of what happened at the hospital.

My neck was in a collar thing, and people kept shining little flashlights in my eyes and putting me in dark rooms and taking pictures. I did know that my dad was there, and by the time a doctor came into our little curtained cubicle, I was feeling like me again.

"You were lucky," the doctor said. He was little and skinny like Jackson, but his eyes were old and smart. "You came out of that fall with some bruises and scrapes and a cracked rib but no concussion and no need for stitches."

"I can take her home, then," Dad said.

Those were almost the first words he'd spoken since he got there, except for, "Are you all right?" and "Just relax. They're going to take care of you. Relax."

I guessed that was Dad-speak for *We'll talk later about what the Sam Hill you were doing up there.*

"You can absolutely go home," the doctor said to me. "But you need to stay quiet for a few days and take care of that rib. It's going to hurt for a while."

"I can't stay quiet tomorrow," I said. "I have to do a presentation at school. After that, I can stay quiet."

The doctor looked at Dad, but Dad just said, "I'll handle it."

Handle it how? No, really. I couldn't miss the fair.

"It'll be a few minutes before you're discharged," the doctor said. "The nurse will be in."

The minute he'd swished out of the curtain I turned to Dad. Moving like that hurt, but I tried to cover it up.

"Dad, please," I said. "I have to be there tomorrow. It's really important!"

"Mr. Hollingberry?"

Someone was standing outside the curtain, and I recognized her voice, only . . . it couldn't be. Dad went to the curtain and looked out, and then he stepped back and let Mrs. Yeats in.

I didn't even know how I felt about that.

"Are you all right?" she said. Everything on her face was jiggling, not just her chins.

Dad filled her in on my injuries. I pulled the nightgown thing up over my shoulders. Nobody ever bothered to tie it in the back when they did stuff to me, and it kept trying to fall off. Like I wanted to be half naked in front of the principal. And speaking of wearing things, she didn't have on her Gold Country vest. She was actually in jeans and a T-shirt with a softball on it.

"Is it all right if I ask Ginger some questions?" Mrs. Yeats said to Dad. "I'm very concerned about this situation."

"Do you feel like it?" Dad said to me.

No, but what else was I going to do? Maybe it would be better if I told it to both of them. Dad wouldn't yell at me in front of her.

"I had to do a retest on the wall climb so I can pass P.E.," I said. "Coach sent me a note and told me to meet him there after school."

"And did he meet you?" Mrs. Yeats said.

"No. I waited a long time, and he didn't show up, so I might have had it wrong. The note's in my backpack in the locker room, so I can't show it to you right now."

Dad made a twirling motion with his finger. That meant move the story along.

"I tried to go back inside, but the door was locked, and then this guy opened it and told me Coach said to do a practice run and he'd be right out. So I did it, but I couldn't get down, and he never did show up."

Mrs. Yeats held on to her chins for a few seconds. "Excuse me for just a moment, would you?" she said, and she slipped out through the part in the curtains.

"I just did what I was told," I said to Dad.

"Yes, you did."

I waited.

"I've taught you to do what your teachers say and that's what you did."

"So I'm not in trouble?"

"No," he said. "You're not."

"Then please don't punish me!" I said. "Please let me do the presentation tomorrow, and then I'll come home and go right to bed."

He didn't get to answer because Mrs. Yeats came back in. Nothing was wiggling. She looked stiff and grim.

"I just spoke with Coach Zabriski," she said. "He never sent a note telling you to come after school. Was it handwritten?"

"No," I said. "It was typed."

"And not signed?"

I shook my head and then wished I hadn't. Ouch.

"I'm going to need to see that tomorrow. For now, what did this young man look like who told you Coach said for you to do a practice run?"

I described him for her. If I hadn't been all hurty and shaky and desperate, it might have been fun, like being on *NCIS*. Nothing was fun right then. Definitely not the iron look on Mrs. Yeats's face.

"I will get to the bottom of this," she said. "Mr. Hollingberry, may I call you at your work tomorrow once I have more information?"

"Call me at home," Dad said. "I'll be there with Ginger."

My heart crashed. All the way. Down.

That was it then. No presentation. I didn't even ask again, and when we got home, I went straight to bed and tried not to cry because it hurt too much.

A couple of times I woke up in the dark because I rolled over on the wrong side. Both times Dad was sitting beside the bed. More ice. More Tylenol.

The third time I didn't move. I just opened my eyes and saw him in the thin early-morning light, still sitting there with Gandalf behind him, telling us both that all those who wandered were not lost. Dad's lips moved, but no sound came out. Just as I drifted back off, I realized he was praying.

I tried too. *Please, God . . . just, please.*

The last time, when I woke up for good, Dad was at the window.

"What time is it?" I said.

He turned around and came to me. "Time for you to stand up and see how you feel."

I didn't lie and say I was fine. I hurt all over, especially my left side. The Hobbits and their friends rolled down hills and fell off cliffs, and they just got up like nothing ever happened. I was clearly not a Hobbit.

I climbed carefully out of bed. I was surprised that once I stood up, I didn't feel as bad. I could hide the pain that was there because I was used to doing that.

"Let me see you walk around," Dad said.

I did while he watched me. My room wasn't that big, so I couldn't go far. Finally he nodded.

"I ran a hot bath," he said. "You go soak for a little bit, and then we'll talk about this."

I didn't want to say anything to mess it up, so for once, I just did it. The whole time I was in the tub I prayed. I still had a hurting side and a bunch of bruises when I was done, but at least I didn't freak and start bullhorning about how I had to go to school. Maybe like Mrs. Zabriski said, somebody else *had* taken over Ginger.

I put on Dad's bathrobe that was hanging on the back of the door and went to my room. But I didn't go in. I just stood in the doorway.

The bed was made, and my Easter dress was spread out on it next to my costume for the presentation. Except for the green cloak, which was draped over the headboard like it was waiting to be put on the queen.

"Here's the deal," Dad said behind me. "Mrs. Yeats called and she wants us to meet her in her office. Then you do your presentation. Then we come straight home. Understood?"

"Yes, sir," I said. My voice was all trembly.

"Look at me."

I turned to face him. His eyes were baggy, and his freckles looked like they were fading as I watched.

"I'm only letting you do this because I think I know why it's important. But when it's over, you and I are going to have a talk."

A good talk or a bad talk? I wanted to say. But I didn't. This was enough for now. Baby Steps.

The fair was scheduled to start at ten o'clock, and all the sixth-graders involved were supposed to be in the gym at 9:30. At 8:30, Dad and I were in Mrs. Yeats's office, after we stopped at the gym locker room for me to drop off my costume and get the note that was supposedly from Coach. When I got it to Mrs. Yeats, she sent her secretary out with it. Then as she handed me a piece of paper, even her chins looked like they had bad news.

"This is a photocopy of a driver's license," she said. "Is that the young man who told you to go ahead and climb the wall?"

I nodded. That was him all right. He didn't even shave for the picture.

"That's the janitor's assistant," Mrs. Yeats said, "and here's the story he told me."

I wasn't sure I wanted to hear it. Not as hard as Mrs. Yeats was looking, like a suit of armor.

"He said he was emptying the garbage cans near the gym when a girl in a sweatshirt with the hood pulled up ran past him and tried to open the locker room door, but it was locked. He told her she couldn't go in, and she said she had to get a message to somebody from the coach." Mrs. Yeats made quotation marks in the air with her knotty fingers. "He said she was 'freaking out' and begged him to let her in. When he wouldn't, she asked him to deliver the message." Mrs. Yeats shrugged, something I'd never seen her do. "Didn't seem like anything bad to him, he said, so he agreed to do it."

Mrs. Yeats moved from the edge of her desk to the chair beside me. Evidently the story was getting harder to tell.

"I asked him to describe this girl to me, and the only thing he could remember was that she was wearing a hoodie with 'a picture of a guy with wild hair on it and some kind of math problem.'" Quotation marks again. "He said, 'Y'know, that really smart guy everybody has on posters?'" Mrs. Yeats sighed from someplace deep. "He meant Einstein."

I knew that before she said it, and I was already shaking my head.

"Tori Taylor is the only one I know who wears a sweatshirt like that," Mrs. Yeats said.

"I know," I said, "but she would never do something like that. Ever."

"I agree, but I have to pursue this, Ginger."

On the other side of me, Dad coughed. Mrs. Yeats wrinkled her forehead.

"I need to go to my job site and make sure my people are there," he said. "I'll be back in time for the presentation. You have this part handled, yeah?"

Mrs. Yeats nodded. "Yes, I don't think we'll need you for this."

She squeezed my shoulder when she said it. At least she understood, even if she did have to "pursue" it. No dad would get what *this* was about.

"I'll be here," Dad said to me.

He left, and Mrs. Yeats asked her secretary to call Tori down. While we waited, she sat next to me again and smoothed down the gold vest.

"I know something has happened between you and Tori and the girls you were doing so well with a few weeks ago. I watch these things, and I talk to the teachers. You've made a lot of progress, but even I have noticed that you've isolated yourself again." The armor kind of came down some. "Please tell me the truth, Ginger. Could Tori be playing some joke on you? Maybe she's upset because you aren't friends anymore?"

"No!" I took a breath. "No, ma'am. I'm the one who stopped being friends with her, but she understands why. And she wouldn't do that anyway. She's the one who wrote the Code. She just . . . wouldn't."

"I hope not." Mrs. Yeats looked over my head and sighed again. "If it turns out she did, or I can't get to the bottom of this, I'm going to have to pull the Anti-Bullying booth from the fair. We can't have false advertising. Especially if somehow the Code has made things worse instead of better."

There was a soft tap on the door, and Mrs. Yeats told the person to enter.

"I got a note to come see you?" Tori said.

I closed my eyes and hoped when I opened them I wouldn't be there.

"Thank you, Tori," Mrs. Yeats said. "Have a seat here beside Ginger."

She watched Tori sit next to me like we might start a fight right there. All I could think of was how glad I was Tori wasn't wearing her Einstein sweatshirt. In fact, she was dressed in jean crops and frog-green tennis shoes and a top that matched them. She was looking her best for the fair.

"I don't usually pry into students' personal relationships," Mrs. Yeats said, "but I have a reason for asking you, Tori: Have you and Ginger had any issues lately?"

Tori looked at me, brown eyes startled, and why wouldn't they be? I wanted to help her, but Mrs. Yeats said, "Tori? Issues?"

Tori sat up straight in the chair. "The only thing I know is that Ginger seemed like she had some things she had to work out on her own, so she left our group. But we didn't have a fight or anything." She gave a very sure little nod. "We respect her, and she has a right to handle things the way she wants to."

"I see."

"But I miss her."

Tori bit at her bottom lip and blinked fast. Tori hardly ever cried, but she was trying hard not to now.

"So you would have no reason to want Ginger to get hurt."

She stopped blinking and stared at Mrs. Yeats. "No! Why would I? No!"

Tori held out both hands like she was saying, *Ginger, what have you accused me of?*

I shook my head and fought tears of my own.

"Can you tell me where you were yesterday afternoon around four o'clock?"

Mrs. Yeats's voice wasn't harsh or anything, but Tori still must have felt like she was being questioned by the FBI. My heart was slamming, and she wasn't even interrogating me.

"I was at my house," Tori said. "We were getting the rest of our stuff ready for the booth."

"Who was with you?"

"Mitch. Ophelia. Winnie."

"Were your parents there?"

Of course her dad was there. They didn't let Tori have friends over without an adult there.

"No," Tori said. "My mom was working, and my dad and Lydia had to leave unexpectedly, but Dad said we would be okay until six, when everybody's parents came to get them." Tori was talking calmly, but I could hear the clog in her throat.

"I see," Mrs. Yeats said. "You're not wearing your Einstein sweatshirt today. I don't suppose you would with that nice outfit."

"I couldn't anyway," Tori said. "I can't find it."

"You can't find it."

"I took it off in the gym yesterday when we were setting up

the booth first period, and I must have left it. I hope it's still there because my dad checked online last night and they don't make them like that anymore."

Tori sounded wounded. Mrs. Yeats just nodded. I wanted to scream, *What more do you want? She didn't do it!*

"Can I ask what's going on?" Tori said.

"Later," Mrs. Yeats said. "I think that's all I need for now. Can I trust you not to discuss this with anyone?"

"Yes," Tori said.

I tried to catch her eye before she left, so I could at least try to show her that I wasn't the one who accused her. But she went in a hurry without looking at me. She might never look at me again.

When she was gone, Mrs. Yeats got up and leaned against her desk, probably so she could look down at me. I always liked her, and she was nice to me, but right then . . . she wasn't my favorite person.

"Who would go to all this trouble?" she said. "Sending a false note. Trying to make it look like Tori was involved. Someone who knew you well enough to think you'd do whatever you were told by a teacher. Who would that be?"

"I can't make any false accusations," I said.

"But you can tell me what you know."

What I knew was that Kylie and Those Girls were so good at being sneaky I couldn't prove anything they'd done to me or Tori or my dad and my brother.

"Are you still being bullied?" Mrs. Yeats said.

That I knew.

"Yes," I said.

"Then I want you to tell me about it so I can help you." The chins were still. "You see, if it's this insidious—do you know what that means?"

"Like, doing something to hurt somebody, only doing it sort of, stealthy, so nobody knows about it?"

"Of course you know what it means. This is what I don't understand." She spread out both hands. "You are one of our brightest students, Ginger. Too smart to let other people take advantage of you. But you are also intelligent enough to know when you can't handle something on your own."

She waited. I thought about it.

I could tell her about Kylie taking one innocent thing I said about my mom's accident so far, it got all the way to practically telling the whole town my dad was a drunk driver and killed her.

I could. But somehow I knew if I did, my dad would end up losing his big job with Kylie's father. I knew it.

I could also tell her that Kylie was using all of that to control me, to get back at Tori and make her whole anti-bullying campaign look like a joke, just because she wasn't the boss of everyone anymore. But I couldn't prove any of it, so it would just go on and on.

Unless I did something about it. Something where everyone could see it.

"Ginger?"

"Sorry," I said. I looked straight at her. "I'm going to tell you everything."

"Good."

"In the presentation."

"I don't understand."

"Everything that happened is in the story Colin and I are going to tell at the fair. And when we tell it—in front of everybody—you'll know. And I think . . . well, I think something's going to happen. Only, will you make sure Mr. Jett or somebody like that is near the Anti-Bullying booth when it's over?"

Mrs. Yeats sighed. "You are a different young lady than you were when you came here, so I'm going to trust you. But if I don't know more after your presentation than I do right now, we'll be back here in my office, and you will tell me everything you know or even suspect. Agreed?"

"Agreed," I said. "Can—may I go now? I need to get into my costume."

"I'll have someone escort you to the gym," she said. "I don't want anyone bumping your poor rib."

Mr. Devon was my escort, which made everything at least a few notches better. He got me to the locker room without a single jostle. Best of all, he didn't ask me any questions.

When I got in there, though, I didn't know how I was going to get out of my Easter dress without stretching and making my side feel like it was splitting open. I was standing there, probably looking forlorn, when somebody grunted and said, "You want some help?"

So Mitch helped me get out of my dress and hung it up on the hanger my costume was on and hooked it onto the top of the lockers. She also got me into my tunic and jeans and boots and even buckled the belt. By the time we were done, I was breathing like I'd done ten sprints.

"I heard you got hurt. Is it true?" Mitch said.

"Kind of," I said. "Thanks for helping me."

"It's okay. I kind of miss helping you. Y'know, since we're friends and stuff."

She left before I could start to cry. Okay, no tears. I couldn't mess this up. I just couldn't.

Chapter Seventeen

When I got out to the gym, Mr. Devon and Lydia and Colin were waiting for me near the door. The gym was already full of kids who were shorter and louder and wigglier than us sixth-graders, which was saying something. I could feel myself starting to blotch.

"Don't go there, Ginger," Lydia said. "You two are going to kick some serious tail out there."

"Indeed," Mr. Devon said. "You'll be brilliant."

He smiled at us, which was unusual enough, but when he smiled down at Lydia, it was different. Wait, was there something happening with them?

I couldn't think about that right then. I looked at Colin, and my mouth broke the record for how far it could come open.

His silky blond hair was swooped back, and it must have been sprayed into place because it didn't move. He had on a tunic like me, only his didn't have sleeves. They were on his shirt instead and they were white and billowy and made him look like a poet, only tougher, because he was also wearing boots that came up to his knees. With both of us in jeans too, we looked like we belonged together.

"Hi, Frank," I said.

"Hey, Samantha," he said.

"Let's get to our seats," Mr. Devon said. "You're last on the program, so I suggest you don your cloaks at the very last minute." He sniffed. "I think it's going to get hot and malodorous in here."

Yeah, you could already tell that fifth-graders probably hadn't been told about sweat and hormones and deodorant yet. Wait 'til Mrs. Zabriski got ahold of them.

"One thing," Lydia whispered, just as Mrs. Yeats stepped up to her microphone and it squealed. "You have been called to do a very important thing. It's a sacred task, and God is with you."

"Amen," Mr. Devon said.

We sat on the bottom row of bleachers near the door, so nobody really noticed us. There was plenty to see out in the middle of the gym.

Tori's science team did a great job demonstrating something that sort of blew up and made red and blue smoke. The fifth-graders went nuts over that. They were so going to love Mr. V.

Ophelia and her group did a pantomime of the stuff they were going to learn in social studies, while Evelyn and Shelby took turns reading it off. If Ophelia hadn't stolen the show, the kids would've gotten more restless than they were already getting.

Mitch totally dominated the P.E. demonstration, and that got the fifth-graders focused again. Her group did some really complicated basketball drill where you could hardly tell where the ball was, and then they jumped hurdles from the obstacle course and ended with doing a thirty-second workout to music. I clapped until my hands stung.

"You're up next," Mr. Devon whispered.

He put Colin's cloak on him and went off to run the PowerPoint. Lydia stood up on one of the bleachers and draped mine around my shoulders.

"Heed the call," Lydia said.

The music started and we were on.

At first, when the lights dimmed except for the ones on us, the fifth-graders whistled and squealed like they'd never been in the dark before, and I wanted to run. But then there was a lot of shushing, and the first slide came up and Colin started to speak. They fell silent, and they didn't make another sound except to laugh when it was right to and sometimes gasp, and even one time somebody yelled, "Yeah, that's what I'm talkin' about!"

Because Colin and I told and acted the story of Samantha and Frank and every kid who ever struggled to be themselves when the Others didn't get it and tried to hold them back and destroy friendship itself.

We climbed on our boxes and cried out in horror when our old wagon, the only vehicle we had, was destroyed by angry Others. The audience was horrified too.

When the wind whistled rumors up almost to the Heights, we calmed them with our capes and got some applause. That was immediately quieted so they could hear us tell the rest of the story, all the way through, until we took off the cloaks we didn't need to hide in anymore and lifted the thin circles of metal that showed up on the screen as rings coupled together.

They knew we had been lied about, manipulated, and left on the wall below to be dragged down back into falseness—and now they knew that even though the Others still wallowed below, we were free. Free to be who we were.

Our lights went down and the music faded—and the whole gym

went crazy. Mrs. Yeats let them stand up and stomp and whistle and clap even after the big lights came up. Then I could see my Tribelet jumping up and down and throwing kisses to me. Mitch put her hand up like she wanted to high-five me all the way across the gym. And there was Lydia next to Mr. Devon, nodding until I thought all her curls would bounce off—and Mr. Devon squeezing her hand.

My dad was there, too, looking tall and proud beside . . . wait— Jackson? Jackson was there, with his hood off, not exactly smiling but clapping some. When he saw me looking at him, he pulled his hand out of his pocket, gave me a thumbs-up, and stuck it back in.

I looked at Colin, and he was smiling too, but his eyes looked disappointed as they swept over the crowd. I was pretty sure that meant his mom didn't show.

"All right, students," Mrs. Yeats said into the microphone. "That was wonderful. Wonderful. But there is more to come here at the fair, so let's start settling down."

People did, sort of. I looked straight at Mrs. Yeats, and she must have felt it because she found me with her eyes.

I made an *O* with my fingers and thumb, a question on my face. She smiled and nodded.

Yeah. She got it.

That meant something was definitely going to happen now. Maybe not *right* now, but soon. While people were sitting down and shushing each other, I looked for the only group that wouldn't be clapping or bouncing.

Kylie and Izzy and Riannon and Heidi sat near the bottom of the third section, and Mrs. Bernstein was in the middle, between Riannon and Kylie. She talked into Kylie's ear, but Kylie just stared straight ahead, eyes glazed over like she'd just woken up. Oh, but the lip. The lip was headed for the nostrils, and even as I watched, she yelled, "All right! Just leave me alone!"

Right then it all got quiet. There wasn't anybody who wasn't at least looking down to see where *that* came from.

"Next on the program," Mrs. Yeats said, "you'll have a chance to visit the booths."

"Hey," Colin whispered to me from his big black cube.

"Yeah?" I whispered back.

"I think she got it."

I glanced at Kylie again. She was trying to get up, but Mrs. Bernstein said something to her, and Riannon grabbed Kylie's arm and held her there.

I took in air and felt the sharp pain in my side that I hadn't even noticed during the presentation. She got it. Now we'd see if that changed anything. Right now, I was worried about the Tribelet booth.

While the sixth-graders who had jobs were getting to their places, Dad came across the gym to me, and he was actually smiling. Like, all the way smiling.

"You were great, both of you," he said. "Great."

Colin ducked his head and said thanks, and, like he saw what Dad wanted him to do, said he'd see me at lunch and moved off to our storyboard. I had a pang of sadness. After today, there wouldn't be any reason for us to have lunch together anymore.

"I learned a lot," Dad said.

When was I going to stop being flabbergasted by the things he said?

"We'll talk about that later. Let's go home. I want you to get to bed."

"May I just talk to my friends for a few minutes?" I said. "I'll change and talk to them really fast, and then we can go. I promise. Okay?"

Dad pulled his phone out of his pocket and looked at it. "Fifteen minutes," he said.

That wasn't even long enough. The fifth-graders had an hour to visit all the booths before lunch. If Kylie was going to try something, I hoped it would be at the beginning.

I walked as fast as I could (while still being able to breathe) to the locker room. I had my belt off before I rounded the corner into our locker row, but I ran into the bench when I saw it.

My Easter dress was on its hanger where Mitch put it, but it wasn't the same as when I left it. Right across the front of its beautiful greenness were the words **KMART SHOPPER** in bright pink lip gloss letters.

My beautiful dress that Dad bought me. The dress nobody else had worn but me. The dress that made me look like my mom.

I had just done the best thing I'd ever done, but the meanness and the awfulness still went on.

Not anymore.

Somehow, I got the dress down, took the costume off, and slipped my dress on. It wasn't zipped all the way up, but it was good enough. I put my feet in my ballet flats and pushed my headband onto my hair, and I walked back out into the gym. Slow and with a purpose, my eyes on my Tribelet's booth.

Two fifth-grade girls fell into step with me. "You were really good," one of them said.

"Thanks," I said.

They peeled off at our actual storyboard, where Colin was answering questions with a pink face. I kept walking. If anybody saw or whispered about my lip gloss dress, I didn't hear them.

The Anti-Bullying booth was mobbed with fifth-grade girls. Some were reading the big copy of the Code. Some were getting smaller versions from Mitch and Winnie and Ophelia. Some were crowded around Lydia and Tori, and as soon as I got there, I heard them telling their own stories, all at the same time like they just had to get them out.

"May I hand out some brochures too?" I said.

Winnie turned to me and let out a little shriek. Mitch grunted. Ophelia started to throw her arms around me, but I took a step back and said, "I have a hurt rib."

She looked down at me, and her brown eyes took up the whole top half of her face. Her mouth came into a *Who?* but I shook my head.

"You were awesome," a tiny girl with a bright yellow ponytail said to me.

"She was one hundred per*cent* awesome," Tori said.

"These are the ones who are awesome." I swept my hand out over the booth.

"Hey," the tiny girl said. "Why do you have that on your dress?"

I didn't answer her. I just looked across from us at the Spanish booth. Nobody was there except a couple of boys scarfing down Doritos and salsa, and of course Kylie and Those Girls.

Kylie looked like she had been waiting for me to see her. When I did, she stepped in front of the booth and crooked her finger at me.

Like she expected me to come right over for a chat.

"Did you want to talk to me?" I called to her.

She gave me the *Are you the dumbest person who ever lived?* look.

"Whatever you have to say you can say in front of my friends," I said.

I must have sounded pretty friendly because the chatter in our booth didn't stop. I did feel Winnie freeze on one side of me, and I heard Ophelia whisper, "All righty then."

I held my breath, which was painful, until Kylie did exactly what

I hoped she would do. She came straight to the booth and folded her arms and put on the Barbie smile.

"Can I just say you were kind of rude just then, Ginger?" Kylie said.

That quieted the booth down. Every fifth-grade girl in there looked at Kylie and probably thought, *Uh-oh. This is the cool girl.*

"You'll find this out anyway when you come here," Kylie said to them. "But I'll just give you a heads-up: you have to cut Ginger some slack because her mom rode in a car with her dad when he was drunk, and it was really sad, but he killed her. So she and her brother are both mentally disturbed now, and basically you can't believe anything they say." She pointed to our poster. "We just follow the Code and leave them alone. We feel sorry for them."

"Okay, wow," Mitch said. She took a step toward Kylie, but I put out my arm.

Little girls bunched together, and some of them giggled more nervously than Winnie ever did. They actually opened up a path for me to walk straight to Kylie.

"She's going to start in, girls," Kylie said.

"Yes, I am," I said, in the voice I used to think was Samantha but was really me. "I don't know why you decided to hate me and bully me the minute I came into this school, and I don't know why I let you. But just so you know, you can't hurt me. You don't have any power over me. I'll be friends with anybody I want and I'll dress however I want and I'll be just exactly who I am. You can't take that away from me. And even if you threaten my friends or my dad, you can't take away their power either. You can use Twitter and e-mails and text messages to tell people things about my family that totally aren't true. You can even get other people to do your dirty work for you so you don't get caught. You can do all that, and it doesn't change who I am. But it sure shows the world who *you* are."

Dead silence in the booth. I mean, like a tomb. Until some little fifth-grader said, "Was that part of the play?"

"No, honey," Lydia said. "That was for real."

The gym was suddenly full of applause again. For once my bull-horn voice had come in handy because evidently everybody had heard it.

Kylie's face was purple. She waved her hands and shouted, "Wait, wait, wait—listen!"

Heads turned her way.

"You can't prove any of that, Ginger," she said. "I *won't* get in trouble this time." Any minute she was going to inhale her lip.

"I didn't say it to get you in trouble," I said. "I don't care if you do. I just wanted you to know how it is, and I don't need proof for that."

"I think I have all the proof I need."

Mrs. Yeats parted the crowd of fifth-graders like she was walking through a wheat field, with my dad right behind her. She stopped in front of Kylie. Dad held back, but his eyes were smoldering coals.

Mrs. Yeats nodded the helmet head at me. Well, at my dress.

"I believe that's your shade, Kylie," she said.

Kylie stomped her foot. She actually stomped her foot, exactly the way a two-year-old would when she was about to pitch a fit. A tube popped out of her shirt pocket and bounced right at Mrs. Yeats's feet. She picked it up, and I saw that it was the same one Kylie had used on me the day of the makeover. Back when I was somebody else.

"Let's see," Mrs. Yeats said. She held it up to my ruined dress. "Looks like a perfect match."

In a minute we were going to have to collect fifth-grade eyeballs off the floor.

"Mrs. Yeats, is this what you're looking for?"

Mr. Jett joined us and held up a sweatshirt.

Tori's Einstein hoodie.

"Where did you find it?" Mrs. Yeats said.

"In Steppe's locker." He held the sweatshirt out to Tori, but his eyes were bullets firing at Kylie. "I've had about enough of your behavior."

Things happened fast and smooth after that. Kylie was half-carried off between Mrs. Yeats and Mr. Jett. Lydia stood on a chair and suggested the fifth-graders visit *all* the booths, and Mrs. Bernstein put on the sombrero and started hawking the chips and salsa. But before too much else happened, Ophelia jumped up on one of Colin's and my big black cubes and shouted in her best theater voice, "That—that right there that you just saw? That's what you'll learn here about standing up to bullies."

A lot of little fifth-graders looked relieved.

I was pretty relieved myself.

Chapter Eighteen

In the next week, my life changed. Not my *whole* life, but a lot of it. First of all, Riannon, Izzy, and Heidi all got ten days' suspension. Kylie was expelled for the rest of the year, and she would have to petition to get back in for seventh grade, and that would be after she went to summer school to do the last grading period over again.

When Mrs. Yeats told me that in her office, I said again that I didn't stand up to Kylie in the gym that day to get her in trouble.

"I understand that," Mrs. Yeats said. "But it was justified, Ginger." She listed all the things Kylie was expelled for.

Lydia proved, using something called IP addresses, that Kylie got into my e-mail account and sent those nasty letters to Lydia and Tori, pretending to be me. When Mrs. Yeats explained what all that meant, I remembered the day Kylie stood over me at the computer in the library and insisted that I get into my account. That was probably when she got my password.

And spreading the kind of rumors she did about my mom and dad, in school using Twitter, was what was called "defamation of character" and that was against the law. It was up to my dad to decide what to do about what happened *off* school grounds, but he would be allowed to use the proof Mrs. Yeats had if he wanted to press charges.

Kylie also got expelled for destroying my property—my beautiful dress—and for stealing Tori's sweatshirt and impersonating her and setting me up in a dangerous situation with the note typed on paper that matched some in her locker. Not to mention plagiarizing (as in copying) Tori's poem and using me to try to pull it off.

I got the feeling from the way Mrs. Yeats held her chins right then that there was more stuff that maybe I shouldn't know about.

I didn't *want* to know about it. Not having Kylie and Those Girls in school made a gigantic difference, but I wanted to think about the other changes. The really good ones.

Like the day I got back to school after I rested for two and a half days until my rib felt better and Jackson told me to quit fakin' (yeah, he came out of his cave). It was Friday, and I went to the lunchroom, ready to sit with my Tribelet, until I saw Colin sitting alone.

When I went over to him, he looked up and gave me the whole smile. The pink started on his neck.

"Hi," I said.

"Hey," he said. "I brought us some pickles."

"Oh," I said. "You want to eat lunch with me?"

"Well, yeah, unless you don't want to, which is . . . I guess . . . fine."

"No, I do!" I said, before light pink could turn to flamingo. "Just let me do something first."

I left my brown bag there and went over to the Tribelet table. Shelby and Evelyn were with them, and all of them were smothering giggles. Except Mitch, who didn't do the giggle thing.

"What?" I said.

"You should totally sit with him," Tori said. "Seriously."

"Do it," Ophelia said. "As long as you come to Tori's after school for a meeting."

"Come," Shelby said.

Evelyn nodded. The Tribelet was expanding.

I loved it so much.

"Okay," I said. "I have to ask my dad."

"My mom already called him," Tori said. "Didn't he tell you? They had a lo-o-ong talk."

"Was it a good talk or a bad talk?" I said.

"It was about the parents' group my mom's starting," Tori said. "Your dad wants to be in it."

Yeah, like I said, my life changed.

So I ate lunch with Colin, and we didn't exactly say we should keep being friends even now that the presentation was over, but we didn't have to. Not after we decided to do a sequel to Samantha and Frank reaching the Heights on the weekends, just because.

He and I had our last meeting with Mr. Devon that day, which also would have been sad if Mr. Devon hadn't said he wanted us to both be library aides next year during our study hall, *and* one of the elementary schools that didn't feed into Gold Country Middle found out about our presentation and wanted us to do it for their fifth-graders in May. Mrs. Fickus agreed that we should rehearse once a week during fifth period.

It was brilliant.

As for Coach Zabriski, he called me out of sixth period and stood me in the hall outside Mrs. Bernstein's door and told me if I ever got on his equipment again without him or Mrs. Z there, he would own me. Whatever that meant, and whatever it was, I was sure he didn't actually *mean* it. Not after he said, "I guess since you climbed the wall and hung up there for an hour, I should pass you."

"Yes, sir," I said.

"Get back to class," he said. "Oh, and, Hollingberry."

"Yes, sir?"

"You're a brave kid."

He went off whistling without his whistle. I didn't cover my ears.

The two other changes were the things I really, really loved.

One happened that afternoon, when we all met at Tori's with Lydia. Shelby and Evelyn could only stay until five, so we basically gave them a crash course in upholding the Code.

"Maybe we won't have to use it now that Kylie and them are pretty much gone," Shelby said. Her nice lips were not in a bunch. She was cute when she smiled.

"Hmm," Lydia said. "Take a look at the Code."

We all looked at our copies.

"Is there anything on there that says we shouldn't just practice every day, even if there *are* no bullies?"

We all shook our heads.

"Besides," Tori said, "Heidi and Izzy and Riannon will be back before school's over."

Ophelia flopped her braid over her shoulder. "I don't think they'll be so tough without Kylie."

"Whether they are or not isn't the point," Lydia said. "They might not change for a long time. If ever."

"We just change," I said. "Into who we are."

Evelyn stared at me.

"Problem?" Lydia said to her.

"No. I hope this doesn't sound bad, but I just didn't know you were that smart, Ginger."

"That's okay," I said. "I sort of kept that a secret."

After the two of them left, the rest of us gathered around Tori's kitchen table like we always used to, and her chocolate lab, Nestlé, put his head in my lap—sort of like he'd missed me too—and Lydia sat on a big thick book that Tori's father wrote so she could be level with the rest of us.

She folded her fingers in a neat stack. "Is there anything that anyone wants to say?"

"I'm glad you're back, Ginger," Winnie said.

"Totally," Tori said.

Ophelia's eyes got huge. "It was so hard. Sometimes we would just sit here and go, 'Why did she leave us?'"

"Phee," Tori said.

"What?"

"She doesn't need the drama queen version."

Ophelia sighed. "Some other time, when it's just us," she said to me. "I know you appreciate the deep emotions."

"Oh," I said. "I guess I do."

"We should both be in drama club next year. We can when we're in seventh grade."

"Speaking of next year," Mitch said. "Kylie and the Pa—her friends made the cheerleading squad, but they all got kicked off."

"I'm sorry to hear that," Lydia said. "But let's not relish their bad situation."

"It's hard," Ophelia said.

Lydia smiled at us with her orange slice smile. "Nobody said this was going to be easy. We just have to keep trying and praying."

Lydia drove me home, and it was cool to see her high car seat and the special handles she had so she could drive even though she was a Little Person. I didn't focus on that too much though because she had other things for us to talk about.

Well, one thing.

"I think you've completed almost all your steps, don't you?" she said.

I counted them off. "Find a one-line assertive response. Do things to avoid being the target. Find a place for yourself. Stop blaming God and look at what God can do." I looked at her pretty profile. "How did you know I did that last one?"

"It shows on your face. And the way you hold your shoulders. You don't look like you're carrying three people's backpacks anymore."

"Did I look like that?"

"You did. And you're praying?"

"Yes, ma'am. It's different than I thought praying was supposed to be. Colin and I were talking about it, and he prays like I do too."

"Love it," Lydia said. "Now, how about the fifth step?"

I sighed and blew my bangs up. "Love my enemy?"

"That's the one."

"Do I have to do that?"

"Jesus says you do. That's where all the rest of the Code comes from, so we can't leave that out just because it's too hard."

"The Code comes from Jesus?"

"It's all in the Gospels. But don't change the subject. Can you love Kylie?"

"You mean, like be her BFF?"

"I do not. I love her, but I wouldn't trust her any farther than I could throw her." Lydia chuckled. "And that wouldn't be very far, obviously." She pulled up to the downtown stoplight and glanced over at me. "How can you tell that I love Kylie?"

I considered that. "Because you wouldn't let us talk bad about her back at Tori's."

"Right."

"And you would rather see her get changed than get punished."

"Correct."

I was quiet with that until Lydia pulled up in front of our house. Then I said, "I do all that."

"Yes, you do." Lydia unbuckled her seat belt so she could turn sideways to look at me. "There's something else that I'm just going to tell you because you probably can't see it yet. Kylie brought out the best in you in the end."

I thought of myself telling Kylie how it was, there in the booth in my lip gloss dress, without crying or whining or feeling all sorry for myself.

"You see it now, don't you?" Lydia said.

I nodded. "So that means I love her?"

"There's one more part. You need to return evil with good by forgiving her."

"Oh," I said.

Lydia laughed and reached over and patted my hand. "That gives us something to work on. You go in and enjoy your evening with your family. I'll see you next week."

Suddenly I didn't want to get out of the car and go in the house. But I did. I didn't realize I was headed for the other good thing that had changed.

When I got inside, the lamps were on instead of the overhead light and there was a candle burning in a jar on the table and I could smell something amazing that I never smelled before in our kitchen.

Jackson stuck his head out into the dining area. "About time you got home. We were gonna eat this without you."

"What is it?" I said.

"Sit," Dad said. "Are your hands clean?"

I looked. "I guess so."

I sat in the chair I used when we did sit down at the table together and saw that the paper napkins were folded and we were using real plates. Was it somebody's birthday and I forgot?

The amazing smell wafted out of the kitchen and onto the table on a platter in front of me. Three big pieces of meat steamed beside three potatoes wrapped in silver foil and a pile of what I only knew was asparagus because I'd seen it in a magazine.

"Eat this and you get dessert," Dad said.

"I'm not supposed to tell you this, but it's strawberries and whipped cream," Jackson said.

"Big Mouth," Dad said to him. "Let's pray."

We bowed our heads and Dad prayed, and I have to admit I didn't hear all of it because I was in shock. I did get in a silent, *Thank you, God. You really do care about us, don't you?* at the end.

The food tasted even better than it smelled, but I could only eat half of mine because my stomach got full so fast.

"You haven't been eating enough, that's why," Dad said. "That's gonna change."

I didn't want to ruin the mood by asking if we could eat healthy instead of junk food. I decided that could wait until later. After the whipped cream.

We took our dessert to the living room, and that's when things really, really changed.

I expected Jackson to go off to the cave with his plate and Dad to turn on the TV. But Jackson sat on the floor and put the bowl beside him like he suddenly couldn't eat either, and Dad patted the couch beside him for me to sit there.

"Think it's time we cleared something up," he said.

"About what?"

"About your mother and how she died."

I stuck the spoon back in my strawberries. *Don't tell me*, I wanted to say. *If something really awful happened, please don't tell me.*

"Jackson knows this because he overheard me talking to

someone a couple of years ago," Dad said. "Only I didn't find that out until after your presentation."

I looked at Jackson. He shrugged.

"It's time for you to know the truth." Dad put his arm on the back of the couch and scrubbed at his face with the other hand. "There was no one else in the car with your mom that night. I don't think I ever even said that. Somehow you both got that idea, and I didn't do anything to clear that up. It seemed like you would handle it better if it was someone else's fault."

"It was *her* fault?" I said.

She was drinking? No. Not after all this. No.

"She was coming home from work," Dad said. "Late at night, after she worked a double shift. We don't really know for sure what happened. From what the police could tell, she probably fell asleep at the wheel. She hit a tree. Died right away."

I looked down at Jackson again. Tears made little trails down his face, and he didn't wipe them off. Dad had them in his voice. I was the only one who wasn't crying.

Why would I cry? None of the bad things were true. Nobody did anything wrong. God didn't choose for her to fall asleep. She just worked too hard, just like Dad, to take care of us.

Dad nudged my back. "You okay?"

"I am," I said.

"Think now we can move on a little better. Now that's not all balled up in here." Dad tapped his chest. "We can do more things as a family."

"Can I ask a question?" I said.

Jackson groaned. Dad threw a sofa pillow at him.

"Two questions, actually."

"One."

"Even if you get sad again about Mom, you're not going to let Grandma take us, are you?"

Dad stared at me until I thought his freckles were going to pop off. "What in the world ever gave you *that* idea?"

"She did. That day in our old house, when she said she would take us if you didn't get out of your black hole."

"You *heard* that?"

"I was kind of behind the couch."

"What a little sneak!" Jackson said.

Dad put his hand up to him. His eyes were firm. Not mad. Just like, *Hear me and hear me good.*

"Listen to me, both of you," he said. "I had a hard time when your mom died. I still do sometimes. But I will never, ever neglect you so that somebody else can take you away from me. Are we clear?"

"You actually thought that, Freak Show?" Jackson said. "We haven't even seen Grandma in, like, five years."

"Never mind," Dad said. "What's your second question?"

"This oughta be a beauty," Jackson said. But he was grinning, and his voice was relieved. And *I* was the Freak Show?

"Question two," I said. "What are you going to do about what Kylie and her sister did to your van?"

Dad chewed at his freckled lip. "Thought about that a lot. If I tell Mr. Steppe what his daughters did, he won't believe me. Not right now anyway."

"He'd fire you," Jackson said.

"I already have other jobs lined up. Here. In Grass Valley." Dad picked up his bowl and stirred the whipped cream around. "Think I'll wait until it might do some good. That okay with you two?"

"Fine with me," Jackson said. "I like the new paint job better anyway."

Dad looked at me.

"They brought out the best in you," I said.

He nodded like I just said something really smart.

So yeah, that week my life changed. I could tell it from my list of *Things People Don't Know About Me*, because the important people knew them all now. And I could tell it by my list of *Things Other People Think About Me*, because they didn't match what I knew about me, so I could throw it away. And I could tell it from my list of *Things I Didn't Say* because I had said the one thing that mattered.

No, not everything was different now. But what was really different was going to stick. Because what was different . . . was me.

Who Helped Me Write
You Can't Sit With Us

It takes more than just the author (me!) to write a book. These are the people who helped me get Ginger and the Tribelet's story as right as it can be:

Mary Lois Rue, who let me stay with her in Grass Valley and made it come alive for me. She's my mother-in-law, the other Mrs. Rue.

John and Amy Imel, my brother-in-law and sister-in-law, who told me what it was like to grow up in Grass Valley, California. (And fed me wonderful food . . .)

My prayer team—**Janelle, Barb, Lori and her family, Connie, and Crystal**—who prayed when it was hard to write about girls being mean to each other.

My editors, **Amy Kerr** and **Tori Kosara**. (We call her "the other Tori!")

All the people who have written books and made films about the problem of bullying. And all the bloggers and website folks who kept me up to date. We call them the **SNOGS**! (SO Not Okay Group Support)

My fellow J.R.R. Tolkien lovers—**Barb Quaale**, **Janelle Baldwin**, **Joyce Magnin**, **Marijean Rue**, and **Melody Dobbins**—who cheered me on as I read The Lord of the Rings trilogy for the very first time so that those could be Ginger and Colin's favorite books.

Marijean Rue, for letting me borrow a line from her unpublished novel. "I'm mistress of my own tongue, not yours" originally came from her brain!

And especially the **Mini-Women on the *Tween You and Me* blog**, who bravely shared their stories with me. They're the ones who showed me that "sticks and stones can break your bones, but words can break your heart." Come join us by clicking on the *Tween You and Me* blog on my website, **www.nancyrue.com**.

You Can't Sit With Us is only one of three books that will make up the **Mean Girl Makeover** trilogy. If you would like to help with the last book by sharing your story of being the victim of bullying or your experience as a bully, please email me at **nnrue@att.net**.

You can also be part of the solution by joining the SO Not Okay Anti-Bullying Movement. Just go to **www.sonotokay.com**.

Blessings,
Nancy Rue

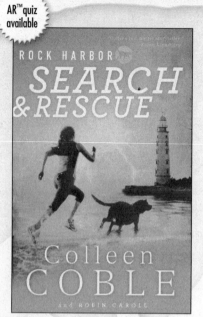

FROM AWARD-WINNING AUTHOR COLLEEN COBLE COMES HER FIRST SERIES FOR YOUNG ADVENTURERS: A MIXTURE OF MYSTERY, SUSPENSE, ACTION—AND ADORABLE PUPPIES!

Eighth-grader Emily O'Reilly is obsessed with all things Search-and-Rescue. The almost-fourteen-year-old spends every spare moment on rescues with her stepmom Naomi and her canine partner Charley. But when an expensive necklace from a renowned jewelry artist is stolen under her care at the fall festival, Emily is determined to prove her innocence to a town that has immediately labeled her guilty.

As Emily sets out to restore her reputation, she isn't prepared for the surprises she and the Search-and-Rescue dogs uncover along the way. Will Emily ever find the real thief?

BY COLLEEN COBLE
www.tommynelson.com
www.colleencoble.com